TERENCE MUNSEY

MARKS of STONE

Book 4 The Stoneman Series

D0840942

Toronto Los Angeles London

This book is entirely a work of fiction. Any resemblance to actual people, places, events, names, incidences, living or dead, is totally coincidental. This work is entirely the product of the author's imagination.

MARKS OF STONE

published by:

Munsey Music

Box 511, Richmond Hill, Ontario, Canada, L4C 4Y8

Fax: 905 737 0208

© 1996 by Terence Munsey

All rights reserved under Domestic and International Conventions. No portion of this book may be copied or reproduced in any form or technology whatsoever, without the written permission of the publisher.

Canadian Cataloguing in Publication Data

Munsey, Terence, 1953-

   Marks of stone

(The stoneman series ; bk. 4)

ISBN 0-9697066-3-4

I. Title. II. Series: Munsey, Terence, 1953-   .

The stoneman series ; bk. 4.

PS8576.U5753M3 1996   C813'.54   C96-930000-X

PR9199.3.M85M3 1996

Library of Congress Catalogue Number 96–94015

First **Munsey Music** original soft cover printing April 1996

Cover design, back note and illustration art © 1996 by Terence Munsey

Cover illustration drawn by MICHAEL STEWART

Manufactured in Canada

<u>Acknowledgments</u>

Thank you **Christina Beaumont** for your editing and comments.

Thank you to **Aunti Tina** who illuminated.

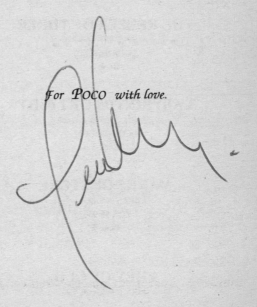

For POCO *with love.*

Books by Terence Munsey in
The Stoneman Series:

THE FLIGHT OF THE STONEMAN'S SON
ISBN 0-9697066-0-X
LCCN 93-93660
Book 1

THE KEEPER OF THREE
ISBN 0-9697066-1-8
LCCN 93-86550
Book 2

LABYRINTHS OF LIGHT
ISBN 0-9697066-2-6
LCCN 95-94007
Book 3

MARKS OF STONE
ISBN 0-9697066-3-4
LCCN 96-94015
Book 4

THEY OF OLD
ISBN 0-9697066-4-2

Book 5

Available at your bookstore

We take the path that beckons. There is no choice, just the *knowing* that it is right.

Chapter 1.

"What do you mean? What Evil? What about Uncle Julian? Where is he? Is he...?" Thiunn did not want to say the word dead aloud, in case it might, as a result, come true.

All three of them were overlooking the chasm, and far below, the river. Only Darla seemed to comprehend what had occurred. They had all stood silently for many moments. After having run up the tunnel after Merm and Julian, they were out of breath, and not willing to accept that the obvious was true. They were in a state of transfer between their awakening awareness and their normal state of being. Their senses were keen, but Eruinn and Thiunn were not able to locate, through their connection within the Magic, the whereabouts or condition of their Uncle. Only Darla still seemed able to inquire into herself, to her ancient knowing. Only Darla, was practiced enough to maintain a longer connection to her awareness within the Magic.

"No. He is not dead." Darla completed Thiunn's hanging sentence, "He is below. He is safe, but the Key is no longer in his control. It has fallen into the river below and must be found before Merm and his *Evil* allies."

Darla was speaking while at the same time, through her linking to the Magic, absorbed in the reconnaissance of the chasm and river far below. She had some greater insight. She was telepathically tuned into the place that gave her this knowledge, whereas Eruinn and Thiunn were not sure what to make of it all. The young Chosen Ones' skills were limited and their retention of any glimpses they had received, short. They knew where they were and what had happened, but were not extremely lucid as to the role played and intervention made by their awakenings in all these events.

"And what are we to do now?" Eruinn added. There was a long silence.

"Ah...find our way down to the river. We must

find your Uncle and retrieve the Key before Lord Merm can." Darla spoke with confidence as she began to become abandoned in thought. It was mystic.

"Lord Merm? Is he alive too?" Thiunn was horrified.

"Yes. He is there." Darla pointed down below. Both Eruinn and Thiunn tried to follow the direction, but were not able to make anything out. It was too far away and it made them dizzy to look that far down the narrow chasm. Darla seemed to be able to see clearly.

The young ones found it hard to believe that Darla could really see anything: *'Only such creatures as the great flying birds of prey could possibly have such visual abilities.'* They independently considered. *'Or maybe it was another type of sight. Maybe Darla saw within her, within the Magic.'* Neither mentioned these views out loud.

"I don't understand." Eruinn was perplexed.

Even though his inner awakenings were feeding him information, it was too complex with all the other events, to take in all at once. Eruinn's thoughts and experience were still centered upon the fight against Merm inside the Cavern of Three. While fighting, the inner beings had been more dominant, now his Jardian self was more in control, and as a result, he was less able to comprehend someone surviving a fall such as this would be, through the canyon abyss to the speck of the river below. The mere image of that fall sent shivers throughout him. This forced him to back away from the opening of the tunnel to the chasm, lest he should accidentally fall over, himself.

"How would that be possible?" Eruinn finished his thought out loud.

Each of the Chosen Ones had different capacities of access to the Magic. Julian had the greatest amount of awakening in order to help him to understand and complete his task. He was allowed more insight and retention of the awakening knowledge.

Darla had the access required to gain and keep the perspective that not only would help with the Stoneman's quest, but also the other dangers that might arise in the future. There was a longer sense of continuity and sharing of awarenesses within the flow of the Magic of the Balance. Her role had always been the role of sentry. As such, she had always better understood the Magic and the Balance. She was aware, in order to protect the Worlds from any initial threat. This was the role she had been following when she had stumbled into all of the recent dangers. She had not been able to deal with the Evil or Lord Merm, but had delivered the message to the right parties in order that together, they may fulfill their obligations.

The young ones were least able to access and retain much of the knowledge of the Magic. They were still apprentices, still young in their sensing. In time they would develop a stronger position, but that was a long way off. Their propensity was much more in the realm of the experiential, an introduction of the actual process of the awakening. The initiation that would provide the primary substructure to rest all subsequent endowments upon.

The hardest aspect for each of them to understand, of all the recent incidents, was the fluctuation of the access to the knowing that each was being given. It came in waves. The awakenings were strongest during the greatest moments of need, and almost immediately after the need had passed, rapidly became weaker. Darla was more capable than the young ones, but even she, after many ages of erudition, found it difficult to accommodate these oscillations. After the depositing of the *Passwords,* and confrontation with Merm in the cavern, the dominance of the awakening within each of the three reverted back to their more normal selves. They were still aware, at a literal level, of the awakenings, but not to the fullest depth of knowing. This created moments of disorientation within them. Moments like now. This current state of confusion would last until the demands of the instant became consistent or evened, in one or another direction of need.

As Darla was of longer experience with the Magic, she was better adjusted to deal with the wave like changes. She was better able to remain focused on a constant line of thought. She could longer hold the understandings of the awakenings within her being. This expertise was a part of her make up and duties as a protecting agent of the Old Ones. The young ones would discover aptitudes of their own in time. Each of the Chosen had these differences according to the specialty of their purpose in awakening. The Old Ones had intricately sewn these seeds as part of their desire to preserve the Balance.

"There has been a great use of the Magic. Your Uncle has become more connected within the Magic in order that he may complete his duty as a Stoneman. I can sense the stirrings within the Balance. 'They' will be with him. He is safe but not out of danger. The *Evil* has reared its head. It has come to the aid of the Gott Lord. It has saved him from the fall." as Darla spoke her eyes had become glossy and taken on a fixed stare out of the Tunnel opening into the canyons. She now had the strange penetrating gaze of a medium:

"There is no understanding The Key is below. We must help your Uncle find it and prevent the *Evil* from obtaining the Magic. That Magic will lead him to the *Passwords of Promise*. Until the Key is safeguarded the *Passwords* are vulnerable. We are to go below."

"How?" Eruinn interrupted.

Darla continued, "There is a way. Under the tomb." Darla suddenly stopped speaking.

Thiunn, who had found Darla's speech and mannerisms odd, nudged his brother to draw these oddities to his attention. Eruinn initially thought it was just an attempt by his mischievous brother to tease him, but then noticed that it was more. Darla had stopped speaking and was staring fixedly outward. The young ones became worried.

"Darla? Darla!" There was no reaction to Eruinn's call. He reached out to grab and shake her shoulder to get her attention.

"Darla. Darla. DARLA." This last time he shouted as he shook. Darla blinked, and her body

seemed to relax. Her knees buckled. It took both
Eruinn and Thiunn to hold her from falling forward into the canyon. They dragged her a length
or so back from the opening. All three fell to the
tunnel floor.

"Darla. Are you okay?" Thiunn asked.

"Yes…" She was a little dazed from the trance
like episode. "I'm fine. I feel a little sick, but it
will pass. We should not stay here long. We must
get down there and see what we can do."

"You said there was a way, through the tomb?
Where?"

"The sarcophagus can be moved to one side,
Thiunn. It covers the entrance to the inner sanc-
tums below. It will lead us to the river. There is an
opening into the river just below the surface. It
will be a good hike." Darla was feeling recovered.

"You two rest here a moment, I'll go back into
the cavern and see." Eruinn was concerned for
Darla.

"No. I'm alright. You don't know what to look
for. If you make a mistake it will release the
beams."

"The 'beams'?" both young ones simultaneously blurted out.

"The beams which protect the entry to the areas
below. If we do not utter the ancient words with-

in the proper time, they will be released and transport us away."

"Away where?" Eruinn looked to Darla with questions that he was not ready to have the answers to. Darla noticed the look.

"There will be time for your answers. Now we must get to the river. Will one of you help me up?" Darla began to rise up with the assistance of Thiunn. "Come along. I will show you."

They made their way back down the tunnel and into the Cavern of Three. All was the same except that the entrance through which they had first entered the cavern, was now closed. The only other way out was through one of the two exits to their right. These were the way that Merm and the Rider had obviously come.

It took them a few moments to adjust from the brightness of the light at the end of the tunnel, to the dimness within the cavern. Gradually, as they adjusted, they each noted the raised dais that pedestaled the sarcophagus. They had not noticed before how perfectly symmetric it stood centrally in the cavern, even its height was of the same radius as all of its other measurements in relationship to its positioning in the Cavern. It was difficult to explain the reason, but they each felt a sense of a greater power involved. The sense that even in the simplicity of the primitive design there was a far greater magnificence nearby. They approached.

Darla was first to stand upon the dais. She cautioned Eruinn and Thiunn to wait as she reverently bowed her head. The chant of Old began:

"Ic noon vra ba, houn gre juk!"

It was in the oldest tongue, the language of the Old Ones. Darla indicated that each young one should repeat after her. They did.

"Ic noon vra ba, houn gre juk! Nuun wra bi nik dwo hee. Ic noon wro vra bo." It was chanted. Darla was a word or so ahead of the repeating by Eruinn and Thiunn.

They voiced more of the same ancient tongue that they had all chanted together earlier with Julian, before he placed the *Passwords* within the coffin, and then were waylaid by Merm and the Rider. Each of them thought of those events as they continued. As the young ones repeated Darla's words, she lifted her head, and looking to each, beckoned them to step up onto the dais. A bright light from above instantly spotlighted them on the raised area.

Darla finished the chant and then moved toward the pedestaled box. It was old and had been carved out of the same rock as the cavern. It was pedestaled shoulder height. Darla peered into it. There was nothing, though before with Julian there had been skeletal remains. She examined the exterior of the container. The sides were smooth. With the touch of her fingers she ran over its hardness. Without breaking contact she caressed its length to the end closest to the Tunnel of Light; again smoothness. Around she went till finally she came to the other end of the coffin. She had come three hundred and sixty degrees, back to her starting place, but facing the end and not the side of the receptacle of Old. Frninn and Thiunn watched patiently. They did not move nor speak. They stood absolutely still. The fear of Darla's earlier warning that the improper tampering with the pedestaled sarcophagus would release a horrible beam; a beam that would transport them they believed to oblivion, filled their being. With the sudden lighting of the dais from above they had become nervous. Though Darla had never explained the danger of the beam, by the tone of her warning at the time, they both deduced that it must be something serious. They both had tensed after the sudden light and carefully watched. Darla paused at the end of the stone tomb.

On the nearest end of the coffin there were carvings. Carvings that had been hidden by the urgency of before. They were the symbols of the language of the Old Ones. The carvings were pictograms and raised from the surface of the smooth rock. She knew what they were. Inside her there was a strong knowing of them. She felt at home. She knew she had been here before this sunrise. Darla placed her hands upon four of the raised carvings.

"Over here. This is it. I will need each of you to place your hands within these two imprints. Quickly." Darla noticed their hesitancy.

Eruinn was first to move toward her, followed by Thiunn. They stood slightly behind her, one to either side. The carvings were impressive.

"There. Eruinn put your hand there." Darla kept her contact with the two carvings, as she used her voice, eyes, and head movement, to indicate the spot. "There. Yes, that's it. Do not remove your hand."

Eruinn did what he was told.

"Thiunn…see the same imprints on this side of my left hand?"

"Yes."

"Copy the way Eruinn is touching."

Thiunn glanced a study of Eruinn's position and copying with the opposite hand in order to fit the carving on his side, placed his left hand firmly upon it. The rock was cool to the touch.

"When I say, push as hard as you can. Then when I shout, take two paces back q u i c k l y. *Understand*?" she stressed the word.

The two nervously nodded in comprehension.

"Good. Here we go. On three. One…two…push!"

They all pushed at the same moment. They felt each of their protruding carvings sink slowly to the smoothness of the end of the box. Then the carvings continued to submerge within the side, so that their hands became more and more buried within the end of the coffin. As this occurred, there played the melody that by now, all of these three Chosen were accustomed to hearing. As it played, the dais spotlight upon them grew in intensity.

"Now! Jump back!" Darla gave the order.

Immediately Eruinn, then Thiunn joined her and jumped back simultaneously. Though they had jumped back, they were all still standing upon the dais at its edge. As if on cue, there began a deep continuous rumbling in the cavern. It was deep underfoot. For a moment the young ones thought that it might be a cave-in. Perhaps this was the danger of the beams of the Cavern. They looked toward and sought confirmation from Darla that all was well.

"Don't look so scared! See…" Darla pointed with her left hand to the pedestaled coffin.

There was a slight fissure at the base where it met the dais. One slab of the dais was separating itself from its center outward into the Cavern. It was sliding away from them. Bit by bit it was separating. The rumbling was the result of its motion. The fissure slowly grew larger. The light above spilled into it. After several moments the sliding of the slab stopped, as did the rumbling. There was a rectangular opening.

"Come on. We're going in there." Darla beckoned.

"There?! How? Where?" Eruinn questioned.

"Come on. It will not remain open for long." Darla stepped forward to the edge of the opening.

"Be careful." Eruinn cautioned, thinking that Darla might fall.

Without listening Darla jumped. Both young ones rushed forward and peered cautiously down. Darla was four lengths lower returning their looks of astonishment.

"Come on you two… hurry, before it closes." Eruinn and Thiunn could just manage to see by the light of the Cavern, that Darla was safe and

20

standing in some sort of passageway.

"Hurry up!" she motioned for them to jump down as she spoke. "Hurry. It will close. You will be left. It's okay. It is the way of the Old Ones."

The rumbling noise recommenced. The large slab was beginning to return to its place within the puzzle of the dais. There was no time to consider.

"Go on, jump." Thiunn was prompting Eruinn.

"You go first." Eruinn was still unsure.

"One of you go first and do it now." Darla was irritated, "NOW!" she bellowed.

Thiunn suddenly awoke from his own anxiety and realized that his brother was frozen with uncertainty. He suddenly appreciated why they would have to jump. It was the only way. It was only a few lengths. There was no point in hesitancy. There was no avoiding their calling. This was all a part of their duty as Chosen Ones. Eruinn or he could not turn back what was meant to be, by refusing to continue onward. It would only make things harder. Harder for each of them, and their Uncle, and the Worlds. This was the next step on their journey. A journey that whether they liked it or not, they were obligated to complete. Remaining in the Cavern of Three was not an option. Thiunn understood his brother's trepidation, but there was no time for discussion or convincing. This had to be done now.

"Well? What are you waiting for?" Thiunn asked.

The slab was moving quickly. It had already closed the opening half way. Thiunn grabbed his brother and jumped. Eruinn was displeased. In moments they were both below and finishing the jump next to Darla. The opening above was less than a length open. If they had waited an instant more, only one would have fit through the opening. Thiunn had understood and was not going to allow them to be separated again on this journey. As they rose to their feet the slab above thundered shut. They were all in complete darkness.

"Darla?" Eruinn called out.

"Where are you?" finished Thiunn.

Though they were not able to see, they felt the confinement of this passageway. They were still next to each other, but a few lengths from Darla. Her response assured them all of their well-being.

"I'm here." Darla answered. There was a ruffling sound coming from the direction of her response.

"What about…" Eruinn was going to say light when the ruffling sound stopped and a dim light suddenly appeared.

"Light?" Darla had been going through her bag

as she stood in the dark. The ruffling sound was her looking for the oblong shaped illuminator, the light of the Old Ones. As she pulled it out of her bag, the illuminator cast out the yellow green glow. Darla was turned to her right and with both hands manipulating the light source out from her bag. As it came more into contact with her touch it grew brighter, though it never reached what could be called bright light. Eruinn and Thiunn could dimly see her twisted shape and then her smiling face. She pulled the illuminator out and with one hand shoved it into the center area in front of them all. They were all within a length or so of each other. The light cast enough glow so that they could make out each other's visage. It was eerie. Their shadows stretched all around and onto the walls of the passageway.

"That's more like it. I had forgotten that you had the illuminator." Thiunn pronounced.

"Me too." Eruinn was out of his 'freeze'.

"This will do us fine here. See how much more bright it is, now that it is back in its place of origin?"

As the Young Ones nodded, Darla taking the illuminator, moved closer to examine the passageway walls which were half a length to the back of them. It was a little difficult to visualize, so Darla put out her hand and brushed against the surface. Eruinn and Thiunn watched.

"Smooth as ice." she muttered in awe.

"What?"

"The walls. Whatever was used to make this passage, it was far beyond what we could do now. They were truly powerful."

"They?"

"The Old Ones. The Ones that made this place and make up a part of us. The Ones who made this illuminator, and the Cavern above. That 'they'." Darla was sardonic, "Who else do you think?"

The young ones did not respond. They had spoken without thinking. Of course they knew these things. Without any more comment Darla turned:

"Come on. This is the way." She moved off without waiting. Eruinn and Thiunn quickly followed. They did not like the dark.

They had not gone far when the passageway suddenly dipped. It became hard to walk along the slanted surface. The diameter of the passageway was larger than the span of their outstretched arms, and the ground beneath their feet was becoming smooth like the walls, after a few more lengths Darla stopped.

"Be careful. It is very steep here." Darla was shinning the light ahead.

The passageway ahead suddenly narrowed to below a length in diameter and seemed to be perfectly circular. She approached slowly with the Young Ones directly behind her. Carefully she reached out to touch the surface of the circular shaft. The circumference was smooth.

"And now?" Eruinn asked as they all were clearly taken aback by what they each silently knew was their next course of action.

"What's at the other end?" Thiunn expressed the concern.

"I think we're going to find out." Darla was not looking forward to what was next. She peered along the passageway. It was too steep and smooth for them to be able to slow themselves after entering the shaft. She thought of turning back, but that was not an option. Somewhere below all of this, was where they were meant to go. She knew this deep inside. She let out a ponderous sigh:

"We must trust in those before. This is the correct way and we must follow it even through here. I don't like the idea, but I feel that we will be safe."

"Well..." Eruinn offered, followed by a brief chuckle of fear.

"Yeah...I agree with Eruinn. The idea of sliding

down through this to who knows what, isn't exactly pleasant. We could get hurt. Then what can we do." Thiunn was right.

"I'll go first. I don't know if it will help. I don't know how far down it goes. You may not be able to hear or know what happens…" Darla leaned into the shaft and shouted hello. It echoed over and over till it eventually faded away. She had hoped this would give some indication as to the length of the shaft. She turned back to face the Young Ones, "It seems pretty long."

"Yeah…"

"Yeah…" both timidly replied.

"I will leave you with the illuminator. Listen carefully, then follow after a few moments. You can't go back. Don't wait too long. Whatever happens, whoever makes it, must go on and find your Uncle. Okay?"

Eruinn and Thiunn nodded in agreement. Darla handed the light to Thiunn, and prepared to enter the shaft.

"Well…This is it."

"Good luck." Eruinn tried to be optimistic in his tone.

"I hope the Old Ones are helping us somewhere. Good luck." Thiunn said his farewell.

"I'll see you two at the end of this shortly."

Darla winked at them, then turned and carefully got into a sitting position within the shaft. She let go and began to slide down. As she slid she called out:

"Don't wait too looooonnnnng." her voice echoed.

Thiunn shined the light after her. He and his brother watched. Quickly Darla picked up speed and went beyond the capacity of the illuminator. She vanished into the dark.

"Will she be okay Thiunn?"

"Yeah. I think we'll all be okay."

They fell to silence and listened to the noise of Darla as she slid farther away from them. It was soon followed by a brief silence then an echo of a scream, not a horrified scream but a nervous scream; the type that you might hear at a Summer Festival from a passenger on one of the rides. The sounds became more and more distant, and the echoes of them intermingled with each other till it was impossible to distinguish voice from sliding noise. Finally it petered out. There were no more sounds from Darla.

The Young Ones held their breath, waited and listened. Nothing. After many moments they were not able to hold their breath any longer.

"Now what." Eruinn asked.

"Do you want to go next, or should I? Thiunn was resolved to the task.

"I'll go. Here take the light."

"Be careful. I won't be far behind." Thiunn held the light and watched his brother enter the shaft. "I love you."

"Me too." Then Eruinn let go. Much the same events as Darla's leaving was experienced by Thiunn. He listened as Eruinn's screams echoed and faded. Again within a few moments there was silence. Thiunn waited a few moments after the last sound was heard and then readied himself. He placed the Illuminator within his shirt, climbed into the shaft, and as he let go pushed himself off and screamed:

" W o o o o o o o o o o o o o o h h h h h h . Wwwwooooooooohhhhh." He was off and sliding into the unknown after Darla and his brother. He prayed he would see them both again very soon.

The ride was incredible. After the initial jitters of the entry and slide had passed, Darla was almost enjoying the slide. The speed was tremendous. Her heart was in her throat and every fiber of her being was enlivened by the thrill of the motion of her sliding from side to side down the shaft. It reminded her of her childhood when her parents had taken her north of Loto and into the smaller hills of the Gott Mountains. There, she had been placed with her father upon a circular sheet with two grips and allowed to slip over the frozen hillside around and around and down. She had always loved it. This was a similar ride.

She had stopped screaming, as she became less afraid of the strange journey The shaft had gone on and on. At first it had been the straight decline, then it changed to twisting and increasing in angles. She had thought that she had even gone through a loop. On and on. The concern of where it ended had momentarily left her as she continued in her nostalgic enjoyment.

Then the shaft had begun to lessen its decline. It began to go into a large spiral. She noted that her speed was slowing. After several hundred lengths of travel, she noted that the surface of the shaft had become less smooth with more friction. She was slowed more. Now her travel was within a comfortable speed for her. She began to sense a type of control. She knew at this speed that she would not come to any harm, regardless of what

surprise might await at the end. The shaft became
less and less smooth. The change did not hurt or
rub Darla. It merely slowed her speed of travel. It
was a strange substance. Almost plant life in
touch, a mossiness, which became thicker and
denser. Her speed became increasingly slower.
She could easily stop at a moments notice.

Darla's attention had been so distracted by the
excitement and her observation of the moss as she
slid, that she had not yet questioned the gradual
illumination of the shaft by the very same moss
that was slowing her. It was not the same plant
life of the passageways of Norkleau, but exuded a
similar light. The shaft began to quickly level, and
up ahead she finally noted a brighter glow. Within
a few more lengths she arrived at the ending of
the shaft as it opened out into a large subterranean
chamber. She came to a stop at the edge of where
the shaft opened and entered the chamber. She sat
with her feet over the ledge of the opening in awe,
admiring the sight.

The chamber was elliptical in shape. The moss-
like plant covered the walls and was giving off a
luminous brightness. Darla noticed that the moss
nearest her was brighter than the moss farther
away. She rose up and walked into the central
area of the chamber. As she walked, the moss far-

thest behind her dimmed ever so slightly and the moss ahead brightened. She concluded that it must be reacting to her presence and drawing from her own energy enough to invigorate it to cast off the light. It was marvelous to have this type of spontaneous reaction. The whole chamber was now lit.

At the far end of the chamber there were two exits. She went to investigate. One to her left was a stairwell. The moss covered its two inside walls, lighting the way. The steps descended as far as Darla could see. She did not enter, but turned to investigate the other exit which was only two lengths away. It was circular in shape. She noticed as she came closer that it was another shaft. Its surface was smooth to touch and was in all ways a duplicate of the entry of the one she had just traveled.

"Interesting." she thought out loud. "This must be the downward route, and the stairs the upward. But where is the other stairwell that would lead up to get to the Cavern of Three?"

She wanted to test her hypothesis by finding another set of stairs. She turned around to view the other side of the chamber, the side she had entered through. The chamber was quite bright. She looked, but could not find another stairwell.

"That's odd. There should be something." She crossed to the other side. At two lengths to either side of the down shaft from the Cavern, she examined the moss covered wall. She was looking for something, but was not sure what.

"Yes… The lever." She recalled the entry to the passages at the Lake of Choices. There would be a lever. She spoke out loud to herself,

"At each beginning the entry is concealed. A lever will open the way." she was speaking as if recalling some old instructions given to her ages ago, but she did not know by whom.

At a point about her shoulder height, the moss was less smooth. Her hand went to touch it. There was something hard beneath the plant life. The moss had become unkempt and grown over the lever and thus concealed it. The lever was a protruding part of the rock. Any passerby would not discern any difference between the rest of the rock of the walls, nor expect to find such an entry. They would not be looking, especially since this was not a place for the uninformed. Not many visitors would find themselves using these passages. These passages were only used by the inhabitants of Tika. It was just the way of the Old Ones to make entry more selective, though not by much, for once the secrets of the shafts and stairs were learnt, travel through-out Tika would be easy, as all passages were constructed on the same basis. These little secrets only helped to prevent wide open entry to any accidental visitor, no matter how remote the possibility of the occurrence.

Darla did not use the lever but smiled, "I understand. Serpents and ladders." She was correct in her hypothesis. She went back to the center of the chamber. She would wait there for Eruinn and Thiunn.

It was not very long thereafter, that Darla began to hear the echoed scream of Eruinn. He was not enjoying the 'ride' and was voicing his complaints all the way down. Unlike Darla he had never enjoyed such rides at the Festival. He, like most Jardians, had never experienced the colder weather sports of the Northern bordering areas, nor had he the desire to have the exposure. He did not like the feeling or surge of the adrenaline in his body as he slid. He preferred to be calm and keep his feet on the ground. When he finally came to the entry of the chamber, it was with a feeling of relief. It was over. He had survived.

"What kept you?" Darla greeted Eruinn.

A disoriented Eruinn rose up out of the shaft. He attempted to take a few steps forward, but fell over. He was feeling dizzy from the slide, and sick. He lay on the soft moss floor.

"That was awful. Never again!"

"You'll get use to it." Darla was in good spirits and found Eruinn's condition humorous.

"Use to it! What do you mean?" Eruinn lifted his swimming head in her direction. Before Darla could answer, Thiunn's cheery voice could be heard approaching through the shaft.

"Here, let's move a little to one side and greet your brother."

As Darla helped Eruinn to his wobbly feet, Thiunn appeared from the shaft into the chamber.

"Wow. That was some ride. Better than the ones at Festival."

"There's going to be more of them." Darla answered Eruinn's hanging question. "It's the way to get to the river. Not bad, uh?"

Darla opened her arms and while supporting Eruinn, gave a huge hug to both after Thiunn had excitedly run to them after his arrival. They were pleased to be safe and together. Their reunion complete, Darla began to explain her discoveries:

"This is the route that those of Tika would take to go up and down. The shafts are a direct route down to many of these chambers. If you stop at a particular chamber and want access to all that is upon that level you take the stairwell. It leads not only to the next chamber up or down, but also through a series of alternate paths beyond each chamber, to the other areas of the level. We will continue to use the shafts and quickly reach the lowest level. From that point, there is a way to the river."

Eruinn and Thiunn did not query Darla's confidence in this knowing. They realized its true source. Eruinn did have one point to make:

"Why can't we use the stairs?" it was said in a pleading tone.

"We must go as quickly as we can. Your Uncle is in great need. We cannot waste a moment. The *Evil* will take advantage of the opportunity." Darla was firm, Eruinn understood.

"Then let's get going." Thiunn released himself from the two and went to the shaft on the other side of the chamber. Without waiting he lifted himself into the shaft and in moments was lost to sight.

"Eruinn. Ready?" Darla softened her voice.

"Okay. Let's go."

First Eruinn, then several moments later Darla, entered the next shaft. They were all on their way to the river.

They went through this pattern nine more times before they reached what Darla had said would be the bottom or river level. They had not stopped to discover more of any level. There was not time.

The final chamber was different from all the others. There was a pool of water and no other exits than the ones leading up. The three weary travelers, now finished with the sliding through the shafts, stood together as they contemplated their next move. The journey from the Cavern of Three had taken most of the sunrise, though they had no idea of the passage of time. They were tired, but their sense of urgency remained.

They watched the pool. It was very still and large. It took up three quarters of the chamber area so that three sides of the chamber were accessible by dry rock, but at the fourth side, the pool of water met the wall. The water was a deep dark blue and very clear. They walked as close as they could around towards the edge to better see where the pool joined with the wall. The glow from the moss was strong and reflected in the blue water, giving it a warm grotto feeling. The pool at this point in the chamber was deeper. Darla bent down to feel the water:

"It's very warm. Here put your hands in."

Eruinn and Thiunn bent down and put both hands in. It was very comfortable. As they waded in the pool with their hands, Thiunn noticed that the pool had motion below the surface.

"Look at that."

Thiunn drew their attention to a small piece of moss that was submerged about three lengths down and drifting toward the place where the chamber wall met the pool. They watched the moss as it moved toward the wall, and then about a length or so nearer to the wall, it was rapidly caught up in a current and pulled farther under. Instead of stopping at the wall, it disappeared.

"There must be a way under the water beyond the chamber." Thiunn mused.

"Yes. Like the pool in the passages near Norkleau." Eruinn understood.

"How like them. The way out of here to the river is under the water through the pool and beyond." Darla was pleased. This was the way, she knew it.

"Should we try it?" Eruinn asked.

"Yes, but this time I will go ahead and see what happens. I will go as far as I can and then come back. That way will be safer." Darla was already taking off her bag and preparing to enter the water. She knew the Young Ones were tired. She would go on and see what lay beyond, then if it was easy enough, they could all pass.

"Be careful." Thiunn was concerned, but

relieved to have a chance to rest before moving on.

"Don't worry. I think this will be the easiest part of our travels today." Darla entered the water.

Eruinn and Thiunn waited and watched from the bank as she swam out to above the spot where the moss has disappeared.

"Wish me luck." She took a deep breath and without hearing their response dove under. Down she went about three lengths and then leveled out and swam to the wall. The Young Ones watched and then saw her disappear under the rock wall. All they could do now was wait and hope that Darla would be safe.

"I hope she will be safe. I don't know what we'd do if she doesn't come back."

"She'll be fine. You worry too much. Remember the underwater passage at Norkleau?" Thiunn was very positive.

"Yes."

"It's probably the same sort of thing. She'll be back before you know it."

"What about U.J.?"

"Uncle Julian! He's alright."

"How do you know?"

"I just feel it, and I trust the feeling.

"But this has taken so long. I never expected it

to be this way when we started from Jard. I thought we would be back by now. Mother must be terribly afraid."

"I know. But we can't worry ourselves about that now. We are Chosen, remember? We can't let everyone down. We have to help and do what is asked of us. Do you think that Lord Merm will stop?"

"No."

"Well then…bear with it. We have to think of everyone, not just ourselves. We can't allow the Gotts to get control of the power of the Key, can we?"

"No. You're right. It's just so much more than I expected. Sometimes I don't think I'm strong enough, and I'm afraid. Afraid of losing any of you."

"I have those thoughts too. But then I think of all those others that without realizing it are in danger, and we are all they have to save them. That gives me more strength. Understand?" Thiunn was soothing to his younger brother.

"Yeah…I do. Just keep reminding me from time to time." Eruinn leaned over and the two brothers embraced. "I'll be alright. You'll see."

"I know, Eruinn. I never doubted it. I'm proud of you."

"Me too." They both hugged a moment longer and then let go. Thiunn searched the water for any sign of Darla as they both sat closely together on the bank, the nearness of each other consoling.

Quite some time passed. The Young Ones were becoming worried for Darla. Surely she could not stay under the water for much longer. Had something gone wrong? They both searched the pool for any sign of Darla's return. A panic set in. What would they do if Darla had drowned!?

"There look! There..." Thiunn spotted a large figure deep in the water. Both brothers eagerly stood up ready to greet Darla. The figure came closer and closer. They examined it as it swam. Closer and closer. It was difficult to make out. Something was different about it. It began to swim the three lengths to the surface. It was moving rapidly and coming closer and closer to the bank. It did not look like Darla. They both jumped back in fear. What was it? Who was it? Where was Darla? Suddenly it broke through the water and into the air of the chamber. It took a gasping deep breath. A hand came out of the water to pull back its hair and clear the water from its eyes. The Young Ones mouths dropped open.

"UNCLE JULIAN?!"

Chapter 2.

Pile after pile was being driven into place. The sound of the hammering echoed above the rush of the river as it attempted to escape its increasing confinement. Beyond these sounds, the sight was remarkable. Everywhere Gott Troopers were organizing work crews. Some slaves were preparing the raw wood logs which had been brought by other slave crews from north of the Burning Forest; some were trimming the shape of each log to fit snugly into the dam that was being constructed out of them, at both ends of the channel; some were delivering more wood to those who trimmed these huge tree trunks into the sturdiest of piles; some were carrying the prepared piles to the next position along the dam; some were working the huge hammer driver, pulling it up to its highest position within its wooden scaffolding using long vine ropes, and then releasing it on command; they repeated the process over and over. Some were holding in place the piles as they were pounded, while they battled against the anger of the merciless river as they worked with the piles: thud...and echo, pause, thud...and echo, pause, thud...and echo, pause, thud...and echo, pause; the hammer was driving each pile in its turn, down. It was slow and rhythmical. There was a pulsating felt throughout the echoed air of the canyon as each pole was being tightly forced into place. After a pile was finally driven into its position, hoards of slaves, directed by loud abusive Troopers, quickly wrapped vine rope around the newest half submerged tree trunks, and onto its neighboring piles. The dam, that together these piles were forming, was nearing completion.

The area was a center of concentration and activity. There was the noise of the whip and brusquely bellowed orders being given to the various crews, by the Troopers in their command. All the sound merged along with the river into one continual, indecipherable whir. It heightened a sense of fear that was looming in the air over both

Gott and slave, as they rapidly worked.

From a distance the whole assemblage resembled a nest of *aunits* scrambling here and there as they managed to manipulate the greatness surrounding them. All the effort and swarm of activity, was diminutive in comparison to the majesty of the canyon and the naked strength of the river as it powerfully fought against their labor. From a distance it was an inspiring struggle. Up close to the slave workers, it was hell.

Progress was being made. Already two thirds of the distance between the western canyon wall and the small island of silt and rock in the middle of the river, was blockaded. It had been most fortunate that at this particular part of the river, a large boulder rested in its middle. Bit by bit the current had naturally deposited the rich soils that were carried amidst its flow around it. Over time deposits had built, till eventually a small island had been established and survived within the flow of water. The island successfully split the river into two separate channels. This had made the job of diverting the flow of the river far more simple. The river would channel more and more of its energy around to the other not dammed side of the island, but at this moment, there was still water filling both sides. The fury of the flow on the eastern branch was increasing, while the water on the west was beginning to slow into a pool. The first stage of the plan was almost complete. After the two lines of piles were in place, one at each end of the island, the water would then be pumped out until there was nothing more than the silt and rocks of its bed. The river would then be temporarily cut off from its path along the island's eastern channel.

There were vine ropes stretching here and there, crossing over the width of the river. They had been either grappled at various angles and heights along both the eastern and western canyon walls, or anchored into the narrow flat rock that lined the river bank. The area resembled an intricate web of some strange arachnid creature. Some ropes were very straight and taut, others formed long drooping curves which occasionally, because of their slackness, were drenched by the rising roll of the river, causing parts of the web to jerk and sway. This movement seemed to give life to the otherwise inanimate rope.

Upon closer examination, it could be seen that the vine rope was also tied and looped together in places, forming avenues that provided a wobbly way to pass items physically by the slaves, from side to side of the river while under the supervision of the sparsely placed Gott Troopers. There was a constant outpouring of activity. The movement had a driven sense of urgency to it, which was accelerated by the periodic sound of the snap and echo of a disciplinarian Gott whip somewhere in the distance. Fear pervaded every slave worker as they heard the whip crack. Everywhere within sight, they responded to the sound by wincing and supplying greater efforts from their weary bodies. Some kept busy at the main focus of their purpose, while others began preparing for the next pile. Still others were scurrying about under the watchful eye of their Gott masters.

The work of the slaves was progressing well. Soon this side of the riverbed would be dry. It had been a difficult challenge. Not just because of the majesty of the task, but because of the treacherous environment where the work was taking place. This part of the river was not designed for habitation or passage. The walls of the canyons were almost vertical in their climb up from the water to the distant heights above. As one starred upward it was overpowering. Vertigo would instantly result from this foolish effort to make sense of this place. There was no sense to be made. It was rough and unpredictable. A few spindly brown twigs, with moldy green foliage, clung desperately to the merciless canyon walls. They steadfastly clung with their finger-like roots to the impregnable rock and were dangling reminders of the fragility of existence in this place. It sent a shiver of fear through the onlookers, which quickly forced them to avert any further attempt to look up. It was better to ignore; to try and cast out the disorienting experience that was caused by the domineering physicalness of the canyon and river. Even looking along the river, with the steep 'V' canyon wall, was upsetting.

In any direction the largeness of the place was beyond the abilities of visualization or comprehension. In this steep narrow gorge, the towering solid rock walls were everywhere. Everything was overpowered by gray and dark. The only brightness was high above in the azure blue sky, but most of that brightness was absorbed by the rock walls. By the time the river was reached only a misty gloomy light prevailed. It was as if even the energy within the light was sucked out as it penetrated deeper into the canyon abyss, till finally exhausted, it fell and was devoured, like the clinging twigs, by the river. All vegetation here at the bottom was gone. Only rock and water existed.

All had been organized quickly, here at the

river. The biggest problem had been the quick finding, and then transporting the tall strong piles from the Gottlands and the area north of the Burning Forest, but it had been done. Access down the canyon wall and then along the river to the specific point where the flow was split into two channels, was permitted by only a precariously narrow edge that skirted along the bank of the threatening unyielding water. In places this edge path became swallowed up by the water and made further passage along the bank extremely treacherous. Occasionally an exhausted slave worker would slip and be lost to the river. Though this slowed the progress of the journey, they would be quickly replaced without much concern. A passing curse was cast upon their soul, by their custodian Gotts, for causing such needless delays by these, *their* careless acts! Slave lives were meaningless. The wooden piles were being used up and more would be needed at the dam site. Conveying these piles along the river would be accomplished regardless of slave losses. There would be plenty more slaves found in order to complete the job.

The slave workers had always been a part of the Gott community. Even after the recent skirmish with the South, most of the slaves had remained in the service of the Gotts. They had been of little concern to the Southern Worlds. The South had only concerned itself with *known* captives, or prisoners of war. The slave that could be identified and rescued. Any that could not be identified or tracked had been left to their misery! It had not been the responsibility of the South to rectify all the abuses of the Gottland. They had been only interested in dealing with, and settling, the most recent invasion by the Gotts along the Northern border.

The South had wanted to quickly put the recent skirmish behind them. Many Southworlder politicians were approaching their time of renewal, and had not wanted their constituent's attention diverted any longer than necessary to the repugnancy of the slave labor, or the reasons why and how the Gotts had risen up against the South so quickly. It was better to leave these things alone and quickly resolve the issue. The sooner it was resolved, the politicians had believed, the sooner it would be completely forgotten, and each incumbent then could claim that their own wisdom and abilities, had helped settle the skirmish. The fear of being too lenient and appeasing of the Gotts, thereby paving the way for a repeating of their invasion at some point in the near future, had been to everyone, unconscionable. A settlement had been arrived upon as quickly as the skirmish had ended. Every other detail or concern had been downplayed by the Southworlder politicians to the inhabitants of their Worlds. They focused only on the fact that the Gotts had been beaten back to their homeland, by the South in its military prowess with remarkable speed and efficiency. The matter had been resolved. They could all rejoice and return to normalcy. As long as the Gotts kept out of the South, and did not bother the inhabitants or any travelers within those boundaries, then they were free to do whatever they wished. The South would not interfere. It had all been agreed, by all parties. The Gotts would be careful to follow these terms with the South. They did not want to rouse any more anxiety.

Fighting with the South was no longer a priority. Lord Merm had realized after his failure to obtain the Key from the thieves, and then overwhelm the South, that another tact must be taken. He had decided to again enlist the Riders and go after the thieves of the Key himself. That small party would draw no attention. As the South had not understood the reasons behind the recent Gott invasion, they would not at be all cognizant of the other greater threats that were still looming over them. Merm still had an advantage. The battle against the South had been lost, but the war was far from decided.

In his mind, Lord Merm had known he would prevail. He would again rise to power and dominate the Worlds. He had realized that his only mistake was to have acted before he had total physical control of the Key. After the conclusion to the recent invasion, he had vowed he would not make that mistake again. He knew that he must have the Key at any cost. Obtaining the Magic of the Key had become his primary goal. It would be done quietly. He would keep out of the South and focus on the far North, in where the South was very ignorant and not interested in watching. Southworlder superstition and fears of these lands was still very strong, just as his had once been. Now, after his trip through the Burning Forest and the Lands of Tika, he knew differently. The only force to fear in these lands of the North would be his and the Gott Troops. They would be the repugnant power, but this fact did not matter to the South now. They were happy with their settlement, and willing again to turn their eyes and thoughts away from the North. They had left these lands, as their ancestors had done before after Lord Ho, to their legends and the Gotts.

Even after the recent invasion, the South had still wanted to be returned to their peaceful isolationist lives, and had again appeased the Gotts as long as their activities remained limited to the far North. That was why the settlement to the skirmish had been signed so quickly. The Gotts would not be punished as long as they made reparation to the territories they had invaded, and then promised to remain within the boundaries as originally set by the Peace Settlement of the Separation War. As an assurance, the Jard Guard would increase its patrolling of its border with the Gottland, to prevent being again caught unaware of any violations.

Everywhere north from the Burning Forest and Lake of Choices would again remain solidly under Gott control. This, the South felt, would satisfy the recent Gott quest for territory and keep them busy, allowing the South to resume its own peaceful isolationism undisturbed. These lands would be a great hardship to tame, a hardship which would keep the Gott occupied indefinitely. So with Gott acceptance, the next phase of peace could begin.

Lord Merm had been pleased after all the documents had been signed. Everything was beginning to work out. The South, satisfied with the settlement, had begun to slowly return to their own affairs, paying less attention to the North. Merm had thought these Southworlders timid, and stupid to have allowed such a settlement. He had too easily convinced them of the difficulties he had been having within his lands with all the rivaling factions. He had fooled the South into believing that the whole invasion had been by a renegade faction, and not the mainstream Gott troops. It had been secretly planned, and its purpose had been to discredit and overthrow him from power. He had assured the South that those responsible would be executed.

Merm had also explained that the Gott needed land to control; that it was a part of their very being. Based on this need he could understand the dissension within his land. The Gott were a proud society whose pride had been bruised by the limits of the settlement of the Separation War. It was not against the South that the recent invasion had been made, as much as it had been a statement of their frustration within a harsh settlement, and a greatly weakened Gottland. Merm needed to be allowed to let his empire grow, to give a sense of pride back to his troops, thereby quieting all other factions. He needed the South to allow the Gotts a place to grow and a new challenge to give to those of the Gottland. It was a goal for them to achieve.

The Southern leaders had sympathized and agreed with Merm. They understood the value in this type of distraction. It would keep the Gotts occupied and away from their Worlds. The terms had been rapidly negotiated. The Peace Settlement was signed, and Merm's empire and rule, saved. It had been better than even he had expected. The only cost had been a sub field commander, who was blamed and executed within one sunrise of the signing of the settlement. Lord Merm had felt this would act as a sign of good faith towards the South. Everyone had been appeased. There would be no resistance. Any who inhabited the lands north of the Southworlder borders, would be either already allied with the Gott or would soon become enslaved. In the minds of the South, this was a satisfactory settlement. When the dust settled from the negotiations, Merm would continue his search for the Key and the thieves. Slowly, through whatever inclandestine path that presented itself, he would continue his addictive quest for power. Before the cave-in he had felt so close to realizing this lust for power.

All this time later, and now again he had these thoughts. He recalled the memory of the past events. He recalled that something at that time after the settlement had been nagging away at him to get on with his search for the thieves. In his dreams there had been an increasing intensity to go after the thieves—but where? He had been driven more and more to find the Key but Merm had not known where to begin.

Pushed by frustration and sleeplessness, he had begun his clandestine search by re-examining the Forbidden Books to find any clue as to the whereabouts of...he had not been sure of what, but something. He had believed there must be some overlooked clue that could guide him in the right direction after the thieves and the Key.

Merm remembered how after the settlement, he had begun to pull himself more and more away from the everyday running of the Gottland and more and more into his search for a place to find the thieves and the Key. He had, by default, allowed Rmont to take care of the transition period after the signing of the settlement. He remembered how little he had spoken to or seen Rmont since his recovery from burial in the cavern, and the signing of the settlement, though he had communicated his commands to him often via written notes.

A chill ran through him as he again recalled the

terror of the cave-in. It had almost taken him. It had been a horrible experience. One that was still bothersome to him, along with his obsession of finding the Key. He had needed time to think. He had not wanted the aggravation of affairs of state. Resultantly, rumors had begun to fill the Worlds as to the health and capability of Merm to continue in his position. Many had believed that he was not the real Lord Merm but an impostor; that perhaps the real Lord was gravely injured or worse, was dead. Merm had ignored all these things. He had needed peace. He had needed answers. He had needed to rebuild his strength both mentally and physically after all of the events. The cave-in had been a final straw to his already strained being. His mind again lingered on the terror he had felt there.

It had been so sudden. Without warning the cavern had begun to crumble. Merm had initially presumed that the thieves had also been buried by the wrath of nature in the cavern, but later, after there was no discovery of their bodies, realized that somehow they had not. In fact, he had become suspect of the part that may have been played by them in precipitating the cave-in. Every time he had had an encounter with these thieves, something unexpected had happened. This angered him. Merm had been unable to protect himself in the cavern, and before he had grasped the danger to himself, he had been buried by large pieces of stone into a silent dark tomb—alive. As mighty a foe as Merm was, this small dark confinement was his nemesis.

Ever since his earliest memories, Merm had passionately loathed these conditions. He remembered how as a young Gott he had been locked into a dungeon in Aug Castle as a joke by his 'friends'. It had been pitch black inside that cell. There had been a rotting smell, and the sound of the scavenger vermin that had managed to survive there off the weakened life of those incarcerated. He had called out repeatedly to be let out. There had been only laughter, followed by silence as he had been left to his entrapment. He had had no idea of how big the room was, or if there had been another in there. He remembered how he had tripped over a large lump, and fell on top of something awful and rotting. There had been the noises of the disturbed vermin running away, as Merm had recoiled in fear and revulsion—a decaying dead prisoner—dinner for the rats. He had begun to scream out of control. Then a sound of the opening mechanism had followed, with an angry voice, and the blinding light of outside, as someone had demanded: *'What was he doing in here?'*, and to; *'Get out!'*

Merm hadn't waited to find out more. He had run for the light, and home. The memory still haunted him, and ever since, he had had a phobia about dark small places.

Merm's mind changed and mixed memories. He now recalled how he had sat pinned within his tomb of the cave-in of the cavern. He had begun to relive all the horrors of his dungeon entrapment. He had begun whimpering to himself. Just as many years before in the dungeon, he was in the darkness, not knowing for how long or if this was to be his end. He had begun to imagine all the sounds of the creatures coming to nibble away at his body. He had been powerless in their world.

It was perhaps this feeling of powerlessness that was the real source for Merm's paranoia of dark confinement. Merm knew that without his power he was a weak insipid being, just like the one he had been during his youth. A youth where he had been ridiculed and left out, outcast from the main community. He recalled how it was only after he had been discovered and nurtured by his mentors, that he had begun to change. Gradually he improved his abilities within the political arena, till finally, and ruthlessly, he had developed a bullying strength of power, power of rule, power to dominate, in tyranny. It had been this power that had placed him above all other Gotts. He feared its loss or any reminder of his true pathetic nature without its presence. The cave-in, and his entombment had brought all of these fears back upon him. He had been again weak, and impotent.

At the point within his entombment of the cave-in, where Merm had felt he would break down from his panic, he remembered how he had heard the calls for him from his Troopers, as they had moved the rubble of rocks aside in a desperate search for their Lord. The voices at first had been faint. Merm had called out. After a few more voicings for help, he had heard their response and acknowledgments. Louder and louder their voices had become, till there had come the closer sound of the rocks burying Merm being broken by picks and being removed, then the light of the rescuers and a face; a face of a Trooper calling to his Lord. He had been saved.

All that seemed so long ago now, though it had only been a few sunrises past. Merm let out a sigh. He remembered how he had felt safe in his room in Norkleau Castle after his rescue. The trauma of the cave-in had passed, and the resolution to the South's invasion had resolved beautifully. Now he just needed to find something that could identify the thieves or at least lead him to wherever they might be.

Merm in this memory, had been sitting at his large table within his castle room. The broken wall that had been the escape route for the thieves, was a nagging reminder of the Key's theft and the setbacks that had resulted. His feelings had changed from the paranoia of his cave-in trauma, to a rage against the 'thieves of the Key', and destroyers of his dreams of increased power and tyranny. As he sat angered by these thoughts, he now recalled how he had moved one of the Forbidden Books which had been in front of him away to one side. He recalled how he had seen the empty box of the Key, which had been hidden behind the great book. How he had stretched over and picked it up. It had been so tiny in his large, rough, hairy hand. As he had moved his fingers over the smooth finish of the container he had pondered. *'There must be something amongst all these books to lead him on.'* It was at this time, that Merm had discovered the lead to finding the thieves. It had been upon the container of the Key. He had found the clue to their whereabouts and had secretly sent Rmont to the Riders and he upon his search for the thieves and Key to Tika.

This musing was so real, but Merm was no longer in Norkleau. He was actually at the river, at the site of construction of the dam. That search which he had just recalled had turned to tragedy. Just as the Key was within his grasp in the Cavern of Three, Merm had lost it. He had taken the steps that had pushed himself, the thief and the Key farther away from one another and into the mighty Pass River. But the thief had lost it too. Before Merm had entered the river from his fall, he had seen the Key fall from the Thief's grip and splash into the water. The Key now lay on the river bed below, waiting to be recovered. This had brought Merm back to the canyon.

Merm vividly remembered his fall from the Tunnel of Light and then his splash into the river below. He had been submerged deeply within its darkness. He had felt his old fear of such confining conditions, but in his effort to fight the rapid current and find his way to the surface, he had not lingered long on those thoughts. The pull of the current of the cold river had overpowered him. He had been twisted and turned just as he had been while falling through the air of the abyss. The only difference had been that he was not concerned, while falling toward the river, about suffocating.

Before Merm had entered deep into the water, he had managed to steal one quick deep breath. Then had come the splashing sound as he had cut through and into the surface membrane of water and had continued deeper into submersion. The force of his speed from the abyss had caused him to fall so deep within the river, that he had not expected to have enough breath to survive the struggle within it to get back to the surface. It had seemed like an eternity passed before he had felt completely slowed by the heaviness of the water as compared to the lightness of his atmospheric fall. He had begun to struggle within the grasp of the river to get back to the surface and the world of breathing life. It had seemed an impossibility. He had been helpless to the current. He had begun to panic as he had strained with what he had believed to be his remaining short moments of breath.

Merm was tense and in a cold sweat as he relived these nightmarish moments. His fears of confining situations began to swell forth. Though he was now safe, these memories haunted him still. He wiped away a bead of sweat from his sloping forehead, and sighed before he continued his recollections.

He had struggled and panicked within the

river's current. He could still feel the wetness and see the darkness. The constant roar of the powerful rapid river had thundered through his submerged ears and being. He had pulled at the water in his attempt to rise up to the surface. His eyes had been open, but the vision had been blurred by the water. Tiny bubbles had trailed all around his motions through the water. He had pulled and pulled. As his panic had reached its height, he had begun to slowly realize that he was slowly being returned to the surface, partly through his efforts of pulling through the water, and partly as a result of his buoyancy. He had then swum harder. He had raised his arms upward over his head and in one strong motion had pulled them all the way down through the water to his sides. As he had done so, he had folded up his large legs and then powerfully kicked them down. He had repeated this several times in unison, each time he had made more progress. The excitement of his success had allowed him to exploit his almost exhausted breath. He had been no longer concerned with preserving his use of air. He had begun to make an all out effort to reach the surface. It had been all or nothing. His large Gott lungs had strained, and his mind had screamed out in desperation, in what they had physically known were their last few moments of life. Merm had pulled away at the water. Again. Again. Again. When would it end? He could not last any longer, but he had to. Again. Again. Again. Where was the surface? He had not been able to see. His breath had suddenly expired! His being had shrieked out for release. He had pulled again. Again. Suddenly his arms had pierced through the water / air membrane of the surface. He had kicked with all his energy to push his head through this membrane and into air. Air, sweat air. Though no noise could be heard above the thunder of the rapids of the river, Merm had gasped out a dry raspy call of joy as he had inhaled the surface air. He was alive. He had managed to take two large breaths and then had been pulled under again. This time however, he had been near enough to the surface of the water that he had been able to fight the current, and every eight or ten strokes, got another breath. This had gone on for a substantial time and distance.

Merm had soon realized that he was in the center of the river amongst the strongest current. Though tired he had become less panicked. He had quickly deduced that he must gradually work his way with the current till eventually he had made his way to the bank and complete safety. He

had slowly continued in his efforts to remain sur-
faced, and gradually slip to one side of the river.
It had taken a tremendous effort from his being.
As he had swum, he had wondered how far he had
been taken from his initial entry point by the
river's current. He had tried to get a visual refer-
ence of his position by the canyon walls, but had
found it impossible. He had no idea where he was.
All he had been able to tell from looking straight
up, had been that dusk was beginning to fall. It
would soon be dark. He had wanted to get to the
bank as soon as he could. He had wanted to get
back to the Key.

As he had continued the gradual move towards
the bank, the power of the river had lessened,
Merm had been able to divert some of his attention to other areas than just his survival of the
river. His thoughts had gone to the Key and the
thief. Had the thief survived? Was the Key on the
river bed? Merm had considered the possibilities.
The thief might well be alive, but he too would
have been taken involuntarily by the power of the
river, and would be separated from the Key. It
would take him a long time to get back to the Key.
The Key, not being buoyant, would have drifted a
little, until it reached the river bed. Merm had
considered that it would be within a hundred

lengths of its entry point. A renewed spirit filled him as he had slowly neared the bank. He could still find the Key. He had to hurry and return to find the Key. But how?

The river bank had been very close, Merm had swum harder. The current had become weaker as he had progressed out of its main flow. In a few more strokes Merm had found himself clinging onto a fallen trunk that had been half in the river and half on the bank. He had followed along its length. The water had become suddenly shallow. His feet had touched. He had half swum and half walked. Within a few paces he had climbed from the water and had collapsed face down on to the river's bank. He had lain there exhausted and exhilarated that he was alive. He had rolled on to his back and looked up to the canyon tops and the dark area above that had a few sparkling specks of reflected light suspended in it. This had been the night sky. He had made it. He had fallen over three thousand lengths and been submerged in the great Pass river and survived. He recalled how a smile had formed on his dirty hairy face as he had closed his eyes and fallen into sleep.

Merm again felt the satisfaction of that moment in the past, even from this memory of those events. His face turned to the same smile that he had known then. It brought comfort to him in his canyon headquarters. It had only been a few sunrises before, but now it seemed an eternity had passed. Now he was back at the point where he had initially fallen through the abyss and into the river. Now again he was seeking the Key. Now again he was given an opportunity to possess its Magic. Merm wondered how long it would be before the blocking of this channel of the river would take to be completed, and the search for the Key within its slimy bed, started. He was tired by the obstacles that kept appearing every time he was near to obtaining the Key. Would it happen again here and now? So much had happened since his crawling out from the clenching grip of the river, and his return to this place.

He gazed upon the river. Its majesty was overpowering. He was alone, though everywhere about him were Troopers and slaves busily erecting the piles to dam this river. But he was alone. He was their Commander. There would be no disturbances. His mind became trance like as he drifted back to the memories of his escape from the river.

He recalled how he had awakened from his exhaustion induced sleep upon the rocky river bank. For a brief moment he had questioned at that time, whether this was just a dream, but had soon realized it was not. The memory was vivid. He had been shivery and soaked. He had felt the damp air chill him. He had looked around. The river had been but a few lengths away. His large feet had been still dipped into it. They had been soggy and uncomfortable, just like the rest of his body. The upper part of his body had come to rest upon a smooth boulder out of the water, but he was wet. This had been part of a larger rock that lay just beyond his head. The rock had been slimy and damp. A green colored moss had been parasitically attached to it. Merm had not liked the feel of this slime. To his left had been more rocky shore line which had appeared impassable. To his right more rocks, and what had seemed to be a natural path leading on through the canyon. The roar of the river had echoed everywhere. He had stretched his glance up; up the huge canyon walls, till eventually the clear azure color of the morning sun had been seen above. He had been reassured of his safety. He had lain upon the slime on his back and his vision had drawn upward through the canyon walls. He recollected thinking out loud, though it had not been possible to hear himself speak over the river's thunderous roar.

"Oh," he had sighed, "from one to another." He

had meant from one bad situation to another. "What now?" It had been as if he were speaking out to another, but no other had been there. "What to do now?"

As he lay there, Merm had considered his plight. He had needed to find a way out of there. He had needed to get back to Norkleau. Yes, that was what he had to do. He had to get back to Norkleau and quickly return with whatever was necessary to find the Key. He had remembered that at the point of the river where he had fallen, there had been a small island which split the river into two powerful channels. It had been an island made from solid rock and river silt. Probably a chunk of the canyon wall that had detached from the cliff and crashed into the midst of the river. It was a very large chunk of the cliff that must have fallen, for the river over the time since, had not been able to move it out of its path. He had looked around from his safe position on the bank and seen the island. The river was split into two short channels. It had been in the channel nearest the western bank from which Merm, the thief, and the Key had fallen. It was there that the Key had been buried deep into the river bed. He was not sure how he had known this with such certainty, but he had. He had also known that he could not do it alone. He had to hurry to get help.

Merm had decided to return to Norkleau and get the materials and Troops he would need to dam up one side of the river where the Key had fallen. Then he would uncover it from the dry river bed. Finally, he would be invincible. There would be no one to stop him...or would there? A fear had haunted him, just like his fear of confinement. It had nagged at him, but there had been no time for this, he had needed to get going, to find a way out.

Slowly Merm had pulled his large wet body upright. He had shakily walked to the boulders on the right of the bank, and found, that with a little climb, he had been able to get to a narrow path. He had struggled to climb the rock. After several attempts he had managed to get a footing and had climbed up and away from the river bank. When he had reached the top of the boulder, he had been able to see that the natural path led through a fissure in the canyon wall along to another narrow ledge along the river bank. He had decided to take this path as far as it would take him, hoping that eventually it would lead down the Pass river and on towards the Marshland, and then to his home of Gott. It was to be a tough hike. On he had gone.

After a while Merm had traversed only a few thousand lengths. It had been hard work and he had found the effort exhausting. Just as he had accepted that this path was not the answer to his escape from the river, he had come to a fallen log trapped between the rocks of the river bank. This log had blocked the path. He had to move it. Merm had walked to the log and had grabbed hold of the wood, and had pulled at it till he had unblocked the narrow path. He had dropped the log into the river. It had stayed in place along the edge of the water, having being caught in a circular current. Merm had watched as the log had bobbed and had turned, but had not moved on into the river.

Merm remembered the sight well. He remembered how instinctively he had decided to jump into the water from the bank and grabbed of the log. He would ride the log down the river. It would be the fastest route. Merm had then grabbed hold of the log and had kicked at the water which had brought him into the main flow of the river.

The ride had been fast. Up, down, around, over, under, above. He had held unto the log with arms and legs as it had careened through the choppy water. It had been tough work timing his breaths and keeping his hold. Though he had been near exhaustion, he somehow had managed to raft his way through the river to the sun set. He had not known how far he had traveled, but had noticed that the water of the river had calmed down, soon it had become calm and even flowing. The huge canyon walls had gradually diminished till finally he had floated along the length of the calm river out of the canyon and into trees and marsh. The large log had drifted smoothly. Merm had climbed on top, and while still holding on, had drifted along with the log.

To this point his memories were strong. Then there was a blank period. The next thing he had known he was being yelled at by excited voices. It had been sunny and the land had had a familiarity to it. The log had stopped moving and had banked itself. There had been some bodies hurrying toward him, but his sight had blurred and he had been weak. He had seen the bodies approach. He had heard one, then another speaking to one another as they had arrived at his location, though he had not been able to make out the words, he had suddenly known that these were Gott voices, and his own Troopers.

"Get me... out..." had been all he weakly muttered.

The Troopers had pulled him off the log and had dragged him on to shore, throwing him upon his back, and thereby revealing his shabby uniform and markings of rank.

"Lord Merm?" had been all that he had remembered hearing before he had given into his fatigue and had fallen to unconsciousness.

Again all of this seemed so long ago. From his vantage point now, it seemed as if it had all been just a bad dream, but it hadn't been, because here he was at the very point in the river where all this had started just a few sunrises before. He was back in search of the Key within the river. These were the real memories of actual events that had passed. He bore them deeply.

"Lord Merm. Lord Merm." a voice intruded Merm's memories of the recent events in his life. Merm looked up to see a young Trooper standing nervously at attention awaiting his Lord's command.

"Yes, what is it." Merm's response was gruff.

"The next section is ready for your inspection, sir." the Trooper was very formal. It was obvious that he was taking no chances at being considered rude or impertinent. He was following his orders and reporting.

"Very well. I will be along shortly. Dismissed." Merm took his eyes off the Trooper as he saluted and quickly retreated back to his duties.

Merm had given orders that he was to inspect every aspect of the work of damming the channel after it was completed. He was to be informed before each next phase was started. The Trooper was doing his duty, but Merm was aggravated at having been interrupted during his recall of his escape from the abyss and rescue from the river. He would inspect the work shortly, but now returned his thought to completing the recalling of his deliverance from this river only several sunrises ago. He returned to his memory of rescue from the river:

The Troopers that had found him had been looking for him. After there had been no answer from his castle room a panic was quietly set in motion. No-one had known that their Lord had found the clue to the whereabouts of the thieves and the Key on the empty box and secretly left Norkleau Castle. Even Rmont had been nowhere to be found. The highest ranking Command had suspected foul play and had instituted orders across the Gottland to begin a methodical search for both Merm and Rmont. The orders had been kept confidential and only for the ears of Gotts. No utterance had been made to any other. This had been done for two reasons, one: they had no wish to alert the South of Merm's disappearance; and two: they had not been certain who had been behind his disappearance. The penalty for any revealing of the orders was death. Every Field Commander throughout the Gottland had been made fully aware of the situation. They had been ordered to send out scout Troops to look for anything unusual. They had not been given further details.

The search had been going on for several sunrises when this one small group of Gott Troopers had gone a little too far northwest and had become lost in the Marshlands away from the Gottland and next to the Ice Barrens. They had been arguing amongst themselves, placing blame on each other for their inability to find their way. They had come to rest by a main clearing in the Marshlands where the strength of the Pass river was still influencing the waters, when one Trooper had noticed a strange object drift ashore about one hundred lengths or so up stream. As the other Troopers had continued their arguing this one had become transfixed upon the object. Something about it had drawn his attention. It had appeared to be a tremendously large drift log. This was not uncommon to the Marsh, but this one had been of the largest the Trooper had ever seen. He had been amazed by its size and shape.

It had seemed as if it had an animal of some sort attached to its uppermost area. As the log approached it had become more clear that the shape upon the log was more than just an unusual clump. It was something clinging on. It was a living being—a Gott! The Trooper had broken into the arguing of his compatriots:

"Shut up! Over there! On that drift log."

The others one by one had followed the pointing finger of the Trooper.

"It's just an old log. Don't get so excited." one of the more gruff Troopers blurted.

"No. Look. On the log." the original Trooper who had first sighted the drift log had implored. "There is something upon it."

They all had stood peering at the object as it had drawn closer. Slowly the log had drifted to the bank and it was certainly carrying a passenger.

"He's right. There is something on it. Quick." had said the largest of the Troopers as he had decided to go and get a closer look. He had beckoned them all to follow.

The Troopers had forgotten their predicament at being lost and had rapidly approached the log. Soon it had become clear that there was a being clinging to the log. It had been large enough to be a—a Gott! Yes, it had clearly been a Gott. The

Troopers had scurried into the few paces of water to reach the log and had pulled it along with its passenger, ashore. It was only after they had thrown the almost dead body upon the shore, and seen the rank markings, and heard Merm's muttered command, that they had realized that this was their Lord. They had been exultant at their find, and impatient to return to their Field Commander as quickly as possible.

Within a very short time, the Troopers had found their way back to their Unit, and Merm was being fed and groomed at their Field Commander's Headquarters. There had been many questions. Questions by Merm of the Field Commander's compliment and their readiness to serve. Questions on the Gottland. Questions by the Field Commander, indirectly, as to what had happened to cause the Gott Lord to be in such a place and condition. These questions had been avoided by Merm. He had continued inquiring into the readiness of this outpost to be called to duty. The response had been that they were ready at any moment to respond to any such call. The Field Commander had understood not to push his Lord on the unanswered queries, but it had been clear to him that there was something very suspicious about Merm's presence in this isolated outpost.

"Then notify your Troops we will leave in the sunrise, and bring as many slave laborers as you can."

Merm remembered the shocked look upon the face of the Field Commander as he had given the order. He had told the Field Commander only that he wanted to build a dam and partially block the Pass river at a point not far from here, in the Tika canyons. He offered no other explanation and the Field Commander had been wise enough not to ask. He had merely saluted and had set in motion the orders.

Merm had also requested maps of the far North, and while all the other preparations were being made, located the spot to which they would travel. It was to be a difficult journey, especially with all the Troopers and materials required, but it had been done, and in record time.

The next sunrise, with Merm at the head of the Troop, they had started the return trip to the river canyon and the Key. Along with the Troops had been brought supplies: timber and a large compliment of slave labor. There had been also a number of slaves and Troops left behind with orders to cut and prepare wood piles and to send them along to the designated spot along the river.

Merm, who had been surprised but pleased to discover that a massive search had been put in place to find him, had ordered that no message be sent to Norkleau as to his safe discovery. Originally, when Merm had embarked upon his quest for the thief and the Key, he had not considered that his sudden absence would cause alarm. He had not wanted any more attention to be drawn to him now. He had just wanted to rapidly acquire the Key from the river bed, without any other intrusions or complications by others, Gott or otherwise. The last thing he had wanted was to cause any alert to the South with regard to his actions, actions that might be regarded as hostile. Any knowledge of his movements here in the far North might be seen as preemptory to a hostile mobilization by some in the South, and by others, within his own empire. Knowledge of Merm's plans could be used as an opportunity to further discredit him, and then seize control in his absence. It was safest to leave everyone guessing. Merm had felt assured that his High Command would not have revealed a word of his recent disappearance to any other than the very trusted within their ranks. When he had completed his quest, all would be remedied. He would be even more omnipotent. The orders had been given and the journey begun.

Though the terrain had been harsh, it had been nothing compared to the journey out of the Tika canyon's. The entourage had traveled non stop and by the following sunrise had come atop the cliffs at the spot in the river where Merm believed the Key to be. There had been no easy route to follow, and it was a long way to the river below. All the best skill of mountain climbing had been required on the descent. Dozens of ropes had been flung over the canyon walls and one by one they had descended the cliff, like insects. Eventually, through the series of ropes, Troopers, slaves and materials alike, had found their way to the bottom of this abyss. It had been an horrific episode with six or more slaves lost to the canyon.

That had been only three sunrises ago. Now the work on the dam was almost complete. Soon the river would be blocked, and then the Key found. A chill was in the air.

Merm took a deep breath and finally tore himself from these memories. It was time to do his inspection. He rose up from his seat and placing his hands on his hips surveyed the river and canyon. He stood at the front of his makeshift headquarters which overlooked the construction of the damming of the river. High above him, and barely perceptible to the best eyes, was the passage of light from which the course of events that had led to this diverting of the river, had started. High above him, other's eyes were watching from the circular opening in the canyon wall.

Chapter 3.

Hold the link. Do not let him go."
Everyone was expending more effort
than they had ever done before.
Everything was so close to fulfillment, that they
did not want to lose Merm at this juncture. Dorluc
was adamant about maintaining the Magic to
safely deposit the large Gott into the river. It was
a tricky task. It demanded such a shifting and
manipulation within the Balance, that there could
possibly be other attention drawn to their *Evil*.
Dorluc and Wakan were very aware of the potentialities, but they needed a few strong moments of
Magic. The combined force by all present was
focusing much Magic from each of them. They
could not maintain this level of use for long, out

of their personal limitations and the fear of draining the Magic too noticeably.

"It is almost done. Hold."

All remained linked as commanded. Dorluc channeled their force towards Merm's fall. It was working. They concentrated more, and Merm's fall was cushioned more. The Gott would survive the fall, and then it would be up to him to survive the river. There was a large splash as Merm had entered the water. They all then broke their link to each other and Merm. Then Dorluc released his concentration from the channeling of their combined Magic.

"It is done."

Dorluc was still in the bad temper that had begun during the initial alert to Merm's falling into the abyss. He was angered by the loss of the Key and *Passwords*. They had been so close, yet they had silently slipped through his grasp like grains of sand. He was disappointed and tired. The whole episode had depleted him and his followers of the majority of their strength. They would have to rest and wait till the Magic within the Balance became more even. This would take some time, and Merm would still require help to accomplish his recovery of the Key and the *Passwords*.

There would be great danger to him in the river. The river would attempt to devour him, to stop him from surviving and completing his task. It would not be possible to give him any assistance, without risking too powerful a drain within the Balance. A drain that would certainly be noticed by the Old Ones or their agents. Dorluc was angered by the jeopardy this presented to his plans. He blamed himself and any around him for the oversight that had led to this dilemma.

"Now get out. Do not go far. I will need you again soon."

His followers were not shocked by this treatment. They were used to the frustrations and the mood swings of Dorluc. They accepted like any weak underling would. Dorluc presented the only opportunity for escape. They would not be able to return to corporeal existence without his knowledge and skills within the Magic. They knew this well and took whatever he discharged at them. They had all released their linking and with heads lowered from fatigue and subservience, filed one by one out of the room, before Dorluc's wrath changed to something more lethal.

Dorluc was standing tensely in front of the view screen as they exited. The screen displayed a turbulent scene of Merm being tossed and twisted by the mighty river. Merm was in struggle against this slithery serpent, but this was not seen by Dorluc. His eyes were shut and his visage taut. A great anger was swelling within him. As the last of his followers left, Dorluc swung his whole spiritual body around and started to argue with himself. Instead of one, there were two voices. The voices were of himself and Wakan, who was still merged within Dorluc.

"Why did you do this!"

Dorluc had discovered through merging of thoughts with Wakan the truth of the episode. He had seen the whole influence by Wakan as Merm fought with the thieves and then was directed to chase after the one with the Key.

"This is a breach that may have cost us both. Did you think you could complete this without my help. You know well that you may not access the Key. It must be by one such as me."

"Yes, I have considered finishing this on my own, just as you have. We are of the same type. We expect each other to act and think this way. It is what has kept us both going, trying to return. Do not pretend to be otherwise. It is good that it is now out in the open. It has been too long hidden." Wakan was astute. He knew that this situation could easily have been reversed with Dorluc attempting to sabotage Wakan.

There was a pause. Dorluc also knew this was the case. He had always expected Wakan to betray him, as Wakan had done now, and as he could just as easily have done if the opportunity had arisen. They were the same.

"Your timing was not as good as mine would have been." Dorluc was calming down from the rage of the mishap. "You should have been more cautious. Now we have lost a valuable opportunity. Perhaps the Others are now aware of our existence." Dorluc did not like having this conversation while he had the shared consciousness of Wakan still merged. "Merm will need more help if he is to survive the water."

"Yes. You are right. We cannot risk causing much more drain than has already been caused."

"Then we must also end this merging union until the Magic is settled." Dorluc took advantage of the moment to put an end to the sharing.

"Yes, prepare yourself."

Wakan was also relieved to have appeased the confrontation. He also wanted to be back in his privacy. This premature merge had caused unwarranted harm. He still needed to keep Dorluc as an ally. The sooner they broke their union the better. It would be harder now between them, and the outcome less predictable. After the power of the Key and *Passwords* was theirs, it would now be very difficult to get rid of Dorluc. Wakan would have to make a new plan to rid himself of Dorluc, while it was still a possibility, but that was better thought of after their disunion. Wakan turned his focus to the ancient tongue and as before repeated over and over, growing louder and louder, in a sound that would look like a spiral shape if it could be seen. The words began to blur. The magic chant was said out loud. It came from Dorluc's mouth but two voices in unison were speaking:

~~~~

"Wru ho lik hy fut! Wru ho lik hy fut! Wru ho lik hy fut! Wru ho lik hy fut! Wru ho lik hy fut! Wru ho lik hy fut! Wru ho lik hy fut! Wru ho lik hy fut! Wruho lik hy fut! Wru ho likhy fut! Wru holik hy fut! Wruho likhy fut!

Wruholikhyfut"

Dorluc slowly turned around and around, his turning increased in speed with the speed of the spoken ancient words. As the words became louder the voices began to separate. On the very last word of the incantation at an orgasmic height, there came a brilliant flash of light and the opaque cloud. The two entities were again separate. There was a brief pause and then Dorluc slowly walked away and out of the opaque cloud that was Wakan.

"I will go. Keep me informed." Wakan's image thinned within the cloud and then vanished. The remaining cloud then quickly dissipated and Dorluc was now singularly alone. How much a fool he felt he had been, especially since Wakan had been correct. They were of the same kind. Wakan had done exactly what Dorluc had expected him to do. It was he that had betrayed himself by not being better prepared or on guard, for such an obvious betrayal.

"You will not trick me again." Dorluc spoke to the nothingness of his screen room. He shook his head, but all that moved was the hood that concealed it. His eyes were open and he turned to face the view screen. He was still angered by the events and frustrated as he watched the figure of Merm as it was tussled through the water. *'Should I take the chance…?'* It was a lingering thought as he watched. His right arm was now lifted to his cloaked visage and the right bony fore finger was touching his wrinkled skin where his lips were. He was horrific to look at.

Merm was obviously losing his struggle within the water. The river would not let go its grip. Soon he would drown, and then Dorluc's hopes of escaping his imprisonment would be delayed again for an eternity until another such as Ho, or Merm came along. Given the choice between being discovered within the drain of the Magic of the Balance, and losing this current opportunity, Dorluc decided. He would provide a very small amount of Magic to Merm, just enough to get him to the surface of the river and on to continuing the search for the Key. He could only give a push to any effort already being made by Merm. Similar to the cushioning that had been provided to break the fall, now he would add buoyancy to bring him to the surface and keep him afloat as long as he was on the river. It would be a steady small flow of Magic. Dorluc believed that by keeping it small and constant, the chances of it being noticed as an illicit drain would be less likely.

Closing his eyes again, but this time not in anger, Dorluc concentrated on Merm. He drifted into his dream influence state, trying to find the shaft that connected to Merm within the river. As soon as he found it, he began his drifting journey to Merm. All this only took a few moments. He felt himself in the river in the faintest way. He was a part of Merm, but Merm was unaware of this influencing, partly due to the distraction of his panic and watery struggle; partly because of the very low level of Magic that was being used by Dorluc on this occasion. As Merm continued his fight to survive, Dorluc added his Magic.

It was difficult to determine whether or not this had been enough help to make a difference to Merm in his struggle. Dorluc also implanted deep within Merm's panicking mind the thought that: *'you are alright, you will survive, hold on, fight!'* Then Dorluc terminated this joining with Merm and gradually returned to himself in his view screen room. All of this process had lasted a few brief moments. Dorluc could not risk any more drain within the Magic. He could only wait and hope that the Gott had the wherewithal combined with the influencing, to survive the river.

The Pass River was ancient. It was more than just water. Within it also flowed an essence of

Magic. The many tales that had been created by the ages the inhabitants of the Worlds, just like the tales of the Burning Forest, were exaggerated. The River itself had no 'life' but it did appear to be sentient to the unknowing, by the manner in which it reacted to certain intrusions into its path. In its section closest to its source deep inside the canyons of Tika, it was a mighty unforgiving foe. Farther along its length, it was more an uneven and unpredictable nuisance. It would seem to most that it was a living force that could sense, and resented any entry into it, by becoming violent and deadly to those who entered, but it was not always the case. On many occasions there was no response to any who dared to enter. From these inconsistencies much folklore had been established.

While it was true that the River could sense those of the Magic, it was not true that it was accomplished by an intelligence of its own. It was more a reaction to certain stimuli that caused its response than a premeditated riposte. The River contained a mild charge of the Magic. This had happened as the Old Ones had grown more able in their use of the Magic, and could be likened to the result of a type of pollution. The River acquired a residual amount of the Magic as a result of its origin and proximity to Tika and the Old Ones. The River over time had become charged by the fall-out of the abundance of use of the Magic, in their early time, by those of Tika. Once the polluting effect of their use of the Magic was determined, thereafter those inhabitants of Tika changed their ways and began to better understand the power and purpose of the Magic and Balance. They became, at this point, the Old Ones. No longer were they interested in their selfish personal opportunities, which had resulted in the pollution of their river, but had become zealous in their attempts to discover a greater significance to this Magic that they had stumbled upon.

The polluting of the river could not be undone, nor the other effects that soon became noticed. Some of the plant life within their underground passageways had taken on the quality of lumines-cence. Fortunately the polluting had provided advantages. This had been an accidental fortu-itousness.

The River, through its acquiring of a charging of the Magic, could detect and was attracted to those of the Magic, no matter how large or small their attachment. When it sensed entry by those of the Magic, it was calmed and thereby seemed to allow a peaceful crossing or entry. When others entered who were not of the Magic of the Old Ones, it reacted violently as if a disease had been introduced into it. It would attack the identified agent virulently. The closer one was to the source of the River, the more violent was the reaction in either direction. It also had acquired the ability to discern those of the Magic of good intent, and those of *Evil*. One explanation for this was possibly that there was a difference of some kind between the two within the Magic. Another was that it was by design, a natural 'intuition' or survival instinct, that existed for some as yet not understood purpose.

Dorluc understood all the inherent dangers of the River. That is why he had decided to aid Merm. The manner in which the River reacted was slow, but once it determined the Magical identity of the entrant, was fast to act. At that point because of his *Evil*, Merm would be lost to the River. Dorluc had to act when he did, if he did not wish to cause a greater drain in the Magic. He hoped that it had been early enough to make a difference. He waited and watched the view screen.

As he viewed, Merm continued to pull away at the water. For every stroke that propelled him upward, the responding current pulled and manhandled him backward and down twice as far. It seemed a futile attempt, but Merm endured. He allowed the current to twist away and at the precise point where it weakened momentarily, until the next onslaught, he furiously pulled upward and through the water. Gradually he began to make a little more headway than the river had dragged him back. Dorluc sensed that the Lord of the Gott would again survive against insurmountable odds, just as he had, with Dorluc's help, survived the cave-in at Norkleau.

The sudden reminiscence of Norkleau caused Dorluc to be jarred back to the reality of the Key, *Passwords* and Jardian thieves. He had forgotten during the urgency of Merm's falling through the canyon abyss, that the one thief with the Key had also plunged into the river; that the Key had been let go and independently entered into the water. He knew that the Key, like the thief would be protected by the River, they were both very strong in the Magic. It would rapidly attract the protective fortifying aspects of the water. The Key would be allowed to fall directly to the riverbed without much drift or any affect by the current of the river. The current would calm around the powerful Key giving it safe passage to the bottom, by forming a tiny circular shaft, while all about it the rage of the water continued. The Jardian would also be protected. Dorluc could not affect the power of the river. He had used what Magic he dared in helping Merm. The River would be able to act upon this agent of the Magic untouched by the Magic of the *Evil*. There was nothing that could be done by Dorluc to countermand the natural tendency of the River to protect such powerful instruments of Magic.

Dorluc was however, curious to discover the conclusion of the thief and the Key after their entry into the water. He directed the view screen to locate them both. Within moments the view screen interchanged displays between the Key sinking to its settling on the bottom, and the gradual safeguarding of the thief. Dorluc shook his head in displeasure. The power of the Old Ones was still very active, even this long after their leaving. He spoke out loud to himself:

"How many other contrivances are there still waiting to be triggered. There have been many surprises. More than I was aware existed. Wakan is still needed. He must know of these things. I must learn more of the secrets that have been kept from me. I must be cautious. There is much more here than meets the eye. I must learn these things while I wait."

Dorluc realized that part of the cause of the dif-

ficulties that he was having both with Waken and
the finding of the Key and *Passwords*, were the
many secreted stratagems that lay in place waiting for one such as himself to trigger them into
service by trying to usurp and abuse the Magic of
Balance with the Key and *Passwords of Promise*
Dorluc observed in silence as both the Jardian and
Merm were saved. Merm's domination would no
longer be easy. The elements of surprise were
passed. The chase for the Key was far from over.
It would now be a race. Now that its location was
clearly known by all, it was merely a matter of
who could be quickest in returning to recover it
from the river bed. Neither of the parties would be
able to swim in these waters. The water would
have to be blocked to allow access. Dorluc felt
that Merm had more ability and opportunity to
rapidly achieve this goal. The Jardian was finally
at a disadvantage. Dorluc must make the most of
this luck. After Merm's escape from the water he
would try to convey this plan. It would not require
any drain to the Magic, as it could be incorporat-
ed within the small constant flow that was
enveloping and helping Merm now. Dorluc raised
his hands and spoke:

"Return to the Key. Block the passage of water.
Hurry."

It was simple, but it would find its way into Merm's thought when the moment was right. There was nothing more that could be done. Dorluc turned away from the view screen, and took the ten or so paces to the door of the room and exited. Without him there the room became even more eerie. Mingled amongst the yellow green light of this world, was the reflecting of the light from the view screen as it continued to display Merm's and then the thief's ordeal in the turbulent water.

Chapter 4.

The looking up made Julian dizzy. He returned his view to the river level, and decided to sit a moment. Carefully he knelt down and sat upon the path. He felt a chill as a slight breath of wind blew past him. He was soaking wet. He sneezed, and wiped his nose on his soggy left sleeve. He was becoming more uncomfortable as the moments passed, and as his recovery from his experience of the jump and entry into the river progressed. He was coming back in touch with his normal self. The only difference was the new insights that were now a part of him. With his right hand he brushed his still dripping hair from his forehead and readied himself to raise up to continue his trek. In one quick agile motion he stood up. The dizziness had gone, though he now noted a claustrophobic sensation. He decided not to look up again until he had had a longer period of feeling normal. He turned his attention to the bank pathway.

The path was composed of gravel-like chucks of stone that had probably been formed over the years from the crumbling of the canyon walls above. There was no uniform shape or size. These stones filled and made a narrow pathway about two lengths wide and stretched along the river bank about one length from the river. Following the downward flow of the river away from the giant boulders that split and forced the water into two channels, the path continued about fifty lengths. Julian could see that it abruptly ended at the canyon wall. If he was to travel in that direction he would have to follow the path into the river. He assumed that over time that part of the path had been washed away by a change in the river. That change had corroded away the path. The canyon plunged directly into the dark water making an impasse. The path probably continued a little way beyond that point. Julian preferred not to enter the water again. He did not wish to get any wetter than he was now. He turned his head to face the other possibility.

Going in the other direction, back up the river, the path seemed to be intact for as far as Julian could see in the poor light of dusk. It carefully skirted along the river's edge. In some places the path was so narrow that it was shiny from the wetness of the splash from the river. The choice was obvious to Julian. He would go back up the river. Hopefully he would find a way to reunite himself with his companions. Though he had nothing to base his feeling upon, he felt that they would soon be together.

He started to hike up the path. The river noise canceled out all other sounds. He could not hear his feet as they methodically were placed upon the gravel path. The only sounds that were audible to him were the river, wind and his own pounding heart. The absence of all other confirming noise of his existence heightened his awareness. He once again became paranoid that he was being watched or spied upon. Again his fears turned to the possibility that it was the *Evil* or Lord Merm—or both. *Maybe he was being followed? But how? There was no place to hide on this side of the bank, and it would be impossible to cross the river safely*. He tried to comfort himself with these thoughts. There was nothing he could do. Without the Key he could not become invisible to any 'watcher'. The best action was to proceed along the path and quickly find the others. As he walked, he nervously scanned the area from his peripheral sight. He picked up his pace as carefully as he was able. He did not wish to alert any 'watcher' of his possible awareness of them.

The path was easy to traverse though it zigged and zagged along with the canyon. Soon he had made his way two hundred lengths. Through the exertion of the walk he had generated enough heat to ward off the chill of his dampness and the cool canyon breeze. He was no longer worried about being followed. His concentration became focused more on his footing on the gravel path and its periodic jutting changes. Every little distance his feet unexpectedly became soaked from the puddles of water that lay in the low sections of the path. Julian's curses at these occasions were lost amongst the roar of the water.

The distance from the path to the canyon walls had also noticeably narrowed from his beginning position. Julian could now at this point reach out his right arm and just touch the cool hard rock. The path was getting more narrow along with the space separating canyon wall from river. At this rate there would be no more space for a path within a hundred or so lengths. Julian was confused. He wondered if this narrowing had been a result of the corrosion over time by the river, or if it had been purposely created this way. The uniformity of the path was clearly not that way from nature; from falling stones. This path had been made by someone. It was very old.

Julian was at home here. This was also a strange sensation for him. The farther he traversed the more he began to anticipate the direction of the path and the sights within the canyon. He was going toward something. Something he felt he had done many times before. Not in this lifetime, but before. He was feeling some type of déjà vu. Ever since his leap from the Tunnel of Light, he had felt different. He had felt more; greater than himself. He was trusting his intuitiveness more than he had ever done in his life. He felt a security and deep knowing calm. This befuddled him in his present circumstances, but he did not expend much energy on that confusion. He knew it would work out; that he had a prescience; that he was now connected to some greater purpose. With these sensations going through him, he walked on.

After another hundred and twenty lengths or so, the path, as Julian had somehow expected, abruptly ended. The canyon jutted out and fell deeply into the water forming a small whirlpool about five lengths in diameter, The path ended at the whirlpool. There was no way to continue. There was no way to pass this point. Looking ahead along the river about fifty or sixty lengths, Julian could see the island that divided the water. The river current from here to the island was extremely violent. Though he had no desire to continue through that water, the river drew him closer with its mighty flow. It caressed and numbed his free thought with its roar. He was falling into its grip. Julian shook his head and broke the spell. Instead, he carefully stepped to the edge of path where it fell into the whirlpool and gazed into the water's murky depth.

The whirlpool spun quickly round. This was caused by the jutting canyon wall about six lengths into the main flow of the river. This jutting created the pool which was turned by the force of the river as it passed the wall and spilled into the pool behind it. Over time through erosion the pool had widened.

Julian gazed into the pool. He was looking for something, but he wasn't sure what. There was something special about this whirlpool. As he searched, he wished that the pool would stop its spinning, so that he could more easily see. Magically the force of the water reduced. The river was still connected to him. Within a few moments the whirl had stopped and all that remained was a calm clear pool. The color of the water had also changed within the pool, being replaced by the same hue as the shaft that had carried Julian from the depths of the river to the bank.

Julian could now see a few lengths down into the pool. It was a cavity that was circular. The shape was too symmetrical to be a natural occurrence. The sides, though slimy from the growth of the algae in the water, were very smoothly cut. The pool was deep. Julian wondered what creatures might inhabit this place. He continued to examine the pool. He felt he had overlooked something. As his vision became accustomed to the hue of the water that was emanating from somewhere deep below, Julian noticed that the section of the pool just where the path ended, was different. The smoothness there was blemished. The blemish went straight down as far as he could see. Julian leaned down to touch the first blemish which was just below the surface of the pool. He expected that the algae growth was the reason for the difference.

The water was cool as his hand and part of his damp sleeve went into the pool. He felt the algae. It was a slimy velvet to the touch. He brushed his fingers along the length of it. As he did this, he sensed a faint memory of being in this spot once before. He leaned more of his weight onto his hand and tried to investigate further down. Other than the thin layer of algae underneath, there was solid rock. In shock he drew his hand out from the pool. He had an idea. Placing his left hand into the pool and onto the blemish, he leaned his weight onto it and brought his other hand slowly next to his left. The blemish held him still. The water came half way up his forearms. Satisfied that he was secure, he slowly shuffled his right hand along the blemish away from himself toward the canyon wall. There was a drop. Julian continued to run his right hand along and down. In another half an arms length he felt another blemish. He quickly pulled his right hand back and drew himself out of the pool.

"Stairs." he said out loud. "A set of stairs leading down into the pool. This is an entry point to Tika."

This was what he was looking for. He instantly realized that this was an ancient entry to Tika. He knew that the stairs would lead him downward.

He knew that he would have to take and hold a very long breath; his best breath, a breath that would just run out before he safely reached the other side. This was a way of preventing entry by any, not of the Old Ones, who might for some reason stumble upon the stairs and brave the twisting of the whirlpool. If they tried to follow the stairs and the underwater passage, not aware of what lay ahead, they would soon panic, as their fear of being trapped and submerged in the underwater passageway increased, and their breath shortened. Such a traveler would turn back, or face the prospect of drowning.

For the travelers who were aware of the underwater maze, they would know that within seconds of expiry of their breath, they would come upon a small cavern. There they could rest and gather their strength for the remaining two caverns that stood between the underwater passage and the underground passages that led to the various levels of Tika.

After the first cavern, Julian knew that he must continue to follow the underwater passage to his right. If he took any other route he would be trapped and drowned. These precautions were necessary to stop unwelcome entry. From deep inside he understood that he must enter the pool and find his way back to Tika. All of this knowledge was instantly clear to him. Inside he understood, but outside he was afraid.

Julian sat down on the gravel path facing the pool. The whirlpool remained calm. He was not ready to embark upon another watery path. He sat absorbed and soothed by the majesty of the river. The light at this level of the canyon was now very dim. Soon it would be dark. He sat motionless staring out over the pool onto the river. He wondered where the Key lay, and how it was going to be possible for anyone to get it. He knew that he would not be able to call upon the river to help. It was only responsive for travel. Again this was a new knowing that he held within. There had to be another way.

As Julian sat, he felt sorry for himself. How he hated camping. He regarded any wilderness experience as camping. He preferred to be in the safety of his home in Jard. Though he appreciated that was not possible, the thought of his home relaxed him. He sighed and spoke out to himself. He could barely hear his own voice:

"Oh father, how I wish you were here now. You would know what to do. This is so hard. So hard…"

"Julian. I am here. I am always with you." a

voice came into Julian's head. It did not startle him. He was pleased to have company. Whether the voice was really that of his father or just his own mind playing tricks did not matter. He needed to talk to someone. Someone who could help him to continue on his obligated path.

"Father. What am I to do. There are so many new thoughts in my head. I know I haven't finished what I started, but how can I now? The Key is somewhere out there and the *Passwords*…" He wasn't sure where they had gone.

"Trust in yourself. The journey is almost done. You have the knowledge inside. Trust in your self. Trust in that knowing. You must go into Tika. You must take the *Passwords* back."

"Again? Where will I take them?"

"They are not safe here. The *Evil* knows they are hidden here. Go to Tika. Go to the seventh level, to the Chamber of Signs. There you will find the *Passwords*. Repeat the old words."

"What words?'

"The ones from the Cavern of Three. Then take them. Without the Key they have no real Magic. Go to the Dwellers. Find the Marks of Stone. They will help you."

"What about the Key?"

"Do not worry. The Key will find its way to

107

you. The *Evil* will come to you. All will be together soon." The voice was prophetic in tone. Julian did not question its direction. "You must hurry. The *Evil* is close."

"Yes. I've felt it." Julian was referring to his sense of being watched.

"The *Evil* will find the Key. You must find the Marks of Stone and prepare for the *Evil*. There is not much time. The *Evil* must not find the *Passwords* after it holds the Key."

It was interesting how easy it was for Julian to cause communication with his 'father'. As they conversed he noted how he no longer was amazed, or shocked by the voices. In fact he now regarded them as a normal part of his being. It was as if they had always been there, but until now he had blocked them out. The voices were there to help him. He was not alone. There was a tremendous knowledge planted deeply within himself. He was connected through time to a vast memory of knowledge. Within this knowledge there were many personalities that blended with the knowledge. He was not sure what these were, but he accepted and trusted them. He wondered if it was just the Magic of the Old Ones and his proximity to Tika, or something else.

"Go to the Dwellers. They will show you the

way. Do not waste time. Go!" the voice abruptly ended.

Julian was used to the unpredictable way the voice came and went. He was happy to have been able to speak to it, his father. He understood what he must do. Rising up, he now was energized with new conviction. He stepped toward the pool and carefully began to descend into the water following the slimy stairs. One, two, three, the water was up to his thighs; four, five, six, now he was submerged up to his chest. Seven, and eight, his mouth was just above the water. He stopped on the eighth step. He would need to take a large breath and be prepared for the underwater passage to the first rest cavern. He exhaled and squeezed his diaphragm with his arms across him. He wheezed as he forced his lungs to be as empty as possible. Then after a slight pause he gasped in the largest breath he could. He extended his upper body farther than it would normally go, then held, then exhaled. He repeated this process four more times, treating each as a warm up to the final one last long breath.

On the completion of the fourth intake, Julian descended farther into the pool. He was now submerged and committed to making it through the passage.

The water was not as murky as Julian had expected. The water was very calm. The yellow green hue was bright. He was able to make out the smooth circumference. It was hard to stop himself from floating back up to the surface of the pool. He stretched his arms out to try and get a grip on to something that would help him to submerge. His hands ran across the slimy smooth surface. Nothing. Julian was concerned that he was wasting his precious breath. He was worried that if he did not solve his buoyancy problem soon, he would have to return up the steps and start over. He continued on a few more steps.

At the thirteen step level, his right hand found something extruding from the smooth wall. He grabbed onto it, bringing his other arm and hand to help him hold and pull. He went down two more steps and reached a base. The extrusion stopped at the base level where a straight level passage continued. He would be able to swim from this point. Remembering that he must keep to the right, he pushed off the base step with his legs and sprang into a swimming position. As he kicked and pulled he moved into the passage. He tried to stay to the right side. There was the same yellow green glow from the walls. It was very faint, but it allowed him to see about one length ahead. It was not a focused sight. Everything was blurred. His eyes were not made to give clear sight under water. He could roughly make out shapes, though he could not easily identify what they were. He kept to the course. He kept to the right side and swam on.

Within ten strokes the passage split into a fork. He did not hesitate as he swam to the right. His breath was diminishing. This passage was darker than the first. The water was warm and murky. He swam without much analysis. He was afraid that there may no longer be a cavern in which he could refresh his breath. Perhaps over time it had changed. He swam more furiously. The oxygen held within him was becoming lean. He kept to the right. The passage was straight and level. It seemed to be endless. He was beginning to feel the strain of the lack of enough breath. His heart was pounding into his throat. His eyes were opened wide. He panicked and let out a few precious bubbles of air. This caused him to panic more. He considered going back as he swam, but knew that he would not be able to make it. There was no choice but to go on.

"Trust. Trust." Julian was not sure of the source of these words, as they appeared in his thought, but these words eased his panic.

He swam more deliberately over the next ten or twelve more strokes, hoping that on the next stroke he would find the cavern. But there was nothing. His air was almost gone. His body was screaming for life. At the point where he no longer had any useful breath, something within him gave him the strength to swim on, where any other would have stopped and perished. Another five, six, seven, he was acting now on adrenaline, eight, nine... He saw above him a glow. He pulled and kicked with the very last strand of willpower that he could muster. One, two, he broke through the water and into air. He was elated as he coughed and gasped in the air. His lungs ached, and his head was throbbing. A chill ran through him. It had been a close call. He had almost perished.

The cavern was nothing more than a small air space. It was semi-circular, a length high and two lengths in radius. It resembled a miniature dome. Yellow green light faintly illuminated the space. It was very tight. Julian had to tread water in order to remain in position above the water and in the air. He did not mind. He was happy that the cavern was still in existence and that the air, though stale, was breathable.

After several moments the stress of the initial

passage passed. He was now breathing more normally. Julian noticed that the illumination within the dome from the plants was increasing in intensity. He pulled one arm out of the water and while doubling the effort of the other arm to keep him afloat, reached out toward the moss. There was a very slight change in brightness. The plants nearest to his arm began to glow more brightly. He pulled his arm back.

"Interesting," he mused, "it still works."

The effort of remaining afloat drew back his attention. He was postponing the inevitable. He knew he must continue, and not allow himself to find distractions that would slow his progress to the next passage.

He readied himself for the next assault. He forced his total consciousness to the task at hand, and began his ritual to gather a large breath. Again he made an effort to inhale and exhale as much of the stale air as he could. He was not sure how far the next rest cavern would be; whether it would be closer or farther than the first passage had been. He was also not completely sure how much longer it would be before he would cross the underwater passages and make it to the other side; to the paths and levels of Tika. There was only one way to find out. He must go forward.

On his fourth intake he held his breath, and stopped treading water. He pulled his arms down through the water and drew himself deep into the passage, away from the security of the small rest cavern. It took a short moment for his eyes to adjust to the blurred and more dim vision through the water. He pulled and turned his body as he swam down and found a passage to his right. He entered and swam as strongly as he could, keeping his sight on the alert for the next cavern, whenever it might appear.

The underwater passage was wider in this section. Julian kept close to its right side and swam. He was now more confident about his survival. As he swam the passage darkened, he pulled himself more to the right and rubbed against the wall as he went. There was no slimy feeling. For some reason the plant growth was gone and with it the light. He became nervous but kept swimming and rubbing against the wall to be certain that he remained on course. It was during these moments of darkness that Julian thought he sensed another presence. Not the presence of the voice, but something else. Something that was of the living world. The sense grew within him. Then suddenly without any warning something large and firm bumped into him pushing him firmly against the wall and briefly stopping his swim. It felt like some large water creature. Julian did not wait to find out. He continued to swim again with a great urgency. He wanted to get away from whatever had collided with him. He did not want to wait to discover what it was. He just wanted to get through the passage away from whatever it was, and on to Tika.

After another ten or so lengths the water became lit again. Julian swam for the light. He felt safer in the light. His heart was now pounding from the fright of the creature in the dark, and the strain of his effort. He swam. Just as his breath was coming to an end he found the next rest cavern. He turned up into it and as he broke into its air reserve, let out a cry from the horror of the darkened portion of the passage and the creature that obviously lived there and may be looking for him now. He quickly drew in a few breaths and then holding one, submerged, found, and began swimming through the next passage. There were no darkened areas in this passage. Julian was worried for his safety. He just wanted to get through this ordeal.

As Julian swam, he noted that this passage was getting larger. He soon saw a tremendous brightness about five lengths ahead. The next rest cavern seemed to be very large. He hoped it marked the end of his crossing. He swam into the brighter underwater light, and slowly pulled himself through the water to the surface. As he neared the blurred membrane between water and air he caught sight of something or things standing above and to one side. They had seen him also. There was nothing that Julian could do. His breath was gone and he was not sure of the creature that may be close behind him in the passage. He pulled to the surface ready to face whatever awaited. As he broke through into the air, the water noise and his gasping for breath was interrupted by two young voices:

"UNCLE JULIAN?!"

Chapter 5.

Bould sat entranced. He was in the *dream state*. He was alone and seated on the wood floor in the center of the room high in the tree tops where he had first met and interviewed the Stoneman. Ever since that Outworlder's leaving and the reuniting of his companions with him, Buold had been feeling uneasy. Quei and Thodox had returned and reported the successful completion of the task, but there was still a darkness looming, not outwardly but within. He felt it and was troubled. There was a calling inside him; a warning that he had not yet been able to understand. This was unusual for the all seeing and knowing Head Elder of the Tribe. He had not been able to relax. Even sleep had been in fits and starts. Buold tried to alleviate his apprehension by continuing his normal activities, but the darkness would not leave. The calling was haunting him.

Every morning at this point of the sunrise was for Buold, the dream time. It had always been this way for him. Every Head Elder had had their own special moment when they were most receptive to the dream state. For some it had been late. For Buold, the best moments were always at the early sunrises. It had always been the most tranquil and relaxed time for him. Ever since the appearance of the Outworlders, however, this had changed. There was a constant unsettling feeling to his existence, one that he had been unable to shake or better comprehend. What was going on inside of him?

He sat motionless amidst his home high up in the trees. There were three Blue Bark sticks smoldering. The light smell of their smoke and their sweetness filled the air. It blended in with the natural forest aromas that found their way into the lofty room. He would not be disturbed. This was his time. He breathed in deep long breaths allowing the sweetness to fill his being. He had his eyes closed and was concentrating on emptying his soul of the daily pressures of his position. There was no sound other than the light breeze that was dancing amongst the tree tops. He was in the beginning phase of the dream state. Slowly he lost contact with his physical person. Willingly he was transferring into the dream state, where if he chose, he could leave his body and travel on the wind to wherever his being was directed.

Buold had always enjoyed this process and the sense of the freedom it gave to him. He was pleased to be the Head Elder holding the secret and responsibility to dream travel. The process had always been an easy one for him. It had been an invigorating experience, but this time Buold was aware that it was proceeding differently. He sensed this would not be an ordinary dream. The process was much harder to initiate, and there was still a darkness within a corner of his soul. It was causing him distress and worry. Normally his mind would always be empty of such feelings by this point of the preparation of the dream state. Buold was becoming very uncertain. He felt insecure about committing himself, to letting go and drifting from his body on the wind. There was a great danger nearby. He felt its omnipresence. In spite of his intuition, Buold continued the transference. It was his duty to protect the Tribe, to discover and alert them to any threats that might challenge their continued existence in their secluded dwellings. There was a threat now. The whole forest relied upon his dreaming to maintain its security.

In the past Buold had always controlled the dream state from beginning to end. He was able to make choices, but this time he was being drawn by another greater power. He found he had no choices now that the dream process had begun. It frightened him at being so maneuvered, but this fear was secondary to his mission. He was the Head Elder and must place the safety of the Tribe above his own. He was slowly drawn deeper into the dream state. His awareness of his person was distanced. He could see the room and his body seated upon the wooden floor. He was floating up away from it. He felt the freedom of the experience and at the same time the fear of his being manipulated. He was being pulled away to dream travel, but not of his own volition. The room began to distort as he moved farther up and away. The room seemed to elongate and stretch. Then with a pop sound he was out of the room and away from his body. He was free and traveling upon the wind. He drifted over the trees. Higher and higher till his home was just a speck in the forest.

He was being pulled northward. He observed the world below. Off in the distance he could see the canyons and the Pass River. He was going toward Tika. Why? He had no reason to be traveling that way. It was forbidden. Only the Ones of the City of Sparkle were allowed to enter that land. Why was he being brought here by the dream travel? There was no answer to his thoughts, and there was nothing that he was able to do to change this journey or the progression of the dream. He was carried on northward.

When he had reached the boundary of the zone of Tika as marked by the Pass River directly below, he started to descend upon the wind until he was a few thousand lengths above the river and just at the level of the higher canyons. The speed of the travel was unusually fast. He was moving along and up the river. The sight was overpowering. He could not take it all in. There were huge rugged canyons to either side, which plunged down deep into the chasm that ended in the water below. He felt insignificant amidst this feat of nature. He was soaring, and like a great bird of prey, kept a keen eye on everything that he could as he passed. There was as yet no clue to the meaning or purpose of his journey.

The Pass River twisted and the colossal canyons

magnified these turns by its own size. Bend after bend he followed the twisting that was like a writhing serpent. This went on for many moments. The monotony of the travel was increasing. Why was he being drawn here? Then ahead out from a larger bending of the river path, Buold saw some movement. His eyes swallowed the sight. Was it a herd of animals? He could not make them out clearly. They were far off and appeared only as dark moving specks. Some of the specks were moving large pieces of objects. They looked liked twigs from his vantage point. This was, at least, the assumption made by Buold. He was curious. Why was this happening? What were these 'specks' doing here? This was unheard of in his memory. There were no such animals that he knew of that lived in this part of Tika, if that was what they were.

The distance between the 'specks' and himself was closing. As he came nearer, the speed of his travel slowed. Soon he was high overhead, he began to hover above the 'specks'. Then whatever was controlling him started him in a descent toward the spectacle. The closer he got, the clearer everything became. He was getting more detail. The 'specks' were not animals. They were Outworlders. They were working near the river, at a point where a great island divided it into two furious channels. He was drawn closer. There were many Outworlders here, all of different worlds. They appeared tired and oppressed. Suddenly scattered amongst these beings, he caught sight of a large hairy creature, then another, and another.—GOTTS! He knew them well. They were animals as far as Buold was concerned. They were stupid, dirty, perverse, grotesque beings. As he came closer, he began to make out sounds other than the roar of the river. There was the snapping of whips, and moaning. There were cries and orders. The Gotts were forcing the Outworlders to work.

Buold was hovering directly overhead only a hundred or so lengths away. He was not concerned about his proximity. In the dream travel he could not be seen. As he hovered, his attention was directed to the eastern channel of the river. It was there that the activity below was being funneled. The Gotts were using the Outworlders as slave labor to blockade one channel of the river. A dam was being constructed. It was nearing completion. But for what purpose? Why were the Gotts here? He did not understand. To block only half the channel was pointless, unless…they were looking for something.

Suddenly Buold began to plummet toward the river. He was out of control. He was afraid. Something was very wrong. The darkness within him grew. He sensed that his life was in terrible jeopardy. He felt as if something else had taken control over him. His speed grew meteoritic. Something was pulling him out of the wind. He was going to crash into the water. As a coldness inside gripped him, he instantly forgot about the Gotts. He peered straight down into his being. He saw an image of himself reflected back, twisted and distorted. There was an *Evil* in the eyes of his image; the eyes, though part of his face, were those of someone else. He let out a scream and closed his eyes to block out the image, but it remained. Just as this occurred, his person was jarred by a loud sound. There was a knocking, and a distant voice. These sounds confused him. They were not from this place Knock. Knock. Knock.

"*Buold?*" his named was being called from very far away. "*Buold? What is wrong? Buold? Can you hear me?*" followed by a rapid succession of knockings, "*BUOLD?!*"

With a jolt, Buold found himself instantly back in his body in his tree top room and no longer traveling on the wind. He was perspiring profusely. Half dazed and emotionally spent, he opened his eyes. To his delight the horrible image was gone, he was no longer in his dream state. He was safe. The darkness had subsided and the only images he saw were those of his well defined home. It had been an abhorrent journey, unlike any he had ever experienced. He was numb. He heard the knocking sound again, interrupting this consciousness. He considered its source. The sound came again more rapidly and louder. It was coming from beyond the door to his room. It was his mate who was knocking and calling his name. There was fear in her voice.

"Buold? Are you there?"

"Yes. Yes, I'm here."

"Unlock the door. What is wrong?"

"Just a moment." Buold gathered his senses and tried to calm himself as he rose and made his way to the door. He did not want to alarm his mate. He reached out and unlocked the door, turned the handle and pulled inward. His agitated mate was revealed. She looked at him up and down.

"What is going on, husband? I heard you call out." though she was trying to appear composed, there was the mark of distress still on her face.

Buold did not want to worry her anymore than he needed. He made up a quick reply:

"I...touched one of the Blue Sticks and burnt

my finger." He immediately took and pampered his left hand.

"Let me see."

"No. There is no need. There is no damage."

"But..."

"NO. IT IS FINE." there was irritation and fear in the tone.

"Well..." Myran understood. He did not want to talk about what had caused him to call out. She changed the subject. She would return to what she had been doing before Buold had called out. She trusted her husband. When it was time he would talk. "The drink is ready. Are you coming?"

"I'll be there shortly, thank you."

Myran took hold of the handle and closed the door as she left.

Buold was shaken. He remained standing and staring into the closed door. Never had he gone through such a terrifying dream. He had never before been in a position of harm. He had always been the observer, never a participant. If it had not been for his mate's interruption of his entranced body, he might have perished and the thread that linked his dream travel to his tree top room severed. He might have been permanently trapped within the dream. He sensed that this could have been the case. Why had this happened? He began to analyze the events of the dream.

Someone in this dream travel was showing him the actions of the Gotts, and someone or thing was trying to prevent him from being able to carry that information back. What was so important? Why were they damming up one channel of the river? What were they looking for, or had they found? Buold did not know. He tried to understand. Perhaps the Stoneman had not completed his task? Perhaps...

"Myran." he called to his mate as the pieces of the puzzlement fell into place within him. He grabbed his shirt off the chair and put it on.

"Myran, we must help them. The *Evil* has returned." Buold hurried. He opened the door while he called out and exited. His mate upon hearing the noise was again alarmed and came to meet him in the main room from the kitchen.

"What is it?"

"A great darkness approaches." Buold was absorbed in his urgency.

"What?" Myran did not understand.

"Where is the Srñga?"

"The Srñga?" Myran's confusion was further complicated by Buold's searching for the Srñga.

The Srñga was only to be used during times of crisis. It had never been used in recent memory. It had become more a ceremonial item and symbol of the office of the Head Elder. It was very ancient and had been passed down from Head Elder to Head Elder since the very beginnings of the tribe. In the old times it had been needed to warn and gather the tribe against Outworlders and their axesaws. It was said that it could summon a great Magic, but there was no memory to date of that ever occurring. During the need, three long bursts were blown into it by the Head Elder. Upon hearing the sounds, all the Dwellers were to gather.

"It's there. In its case." Myran pointed.

"Yes, of course."

Buold took several paces across the room to where the small case that held the Srñga, rested. He reverently opened the case and delicately removed the artifact. It was small and bone white. There were intricate carvings over its surface. It was the size of three hand widths. At the end, where it was placed between the lips, there was an ornate silvery receptacle. At the other end was a much larger orifice which shaped and allowed the sound to bellow forth. It was curved so that when it was held to the lips in its correct upward position, the other conical opening was level and just above the forehead. When it was blown it appeared as if the blower was sending a message upward to the heavens.

Buold held the Srñga in both hands outstretched from his body. He turned and without a word proceeded to the main door of his home and out to the balustrade that overlooked the south eastern side of the community. Myran followed, amazed at what she believed was about to happen. Buold walked to the edge and drew the Srñga close to his chest. He closed his eyes:

"Wru nik mun tra Srñga wo!" it sounded prayer-like. Myran bowed her head and waited a length or so behind her mate.

"Ki nik kno do ba wre."

Then opening his eyes, Buold guided the Srñga to his lips. He held it firmly, and drew in a strong breath. Then:

"B——e——e——w——a——h——r——e!" the blow sounding almost like a desperate cry from something of the forest. It lasted as long as his breath. Buold drew another breath. Then again:

"B——e——e——w——a——h——r——e!"

All other sounds of the forest and the Dwellers' homes ceased. It was haunting.

"B——e——e——w——a——h——r——e!"

After the third blow finished, Buold backed away from the edge and dropped the Srñga within his left grip, to his side. He closed his eyes and spoke the ancient greeting:

"It is good to be alive. And with friends."

"And with friends." Myran automatically responded to the litany.

"With friends together, on such a sunrise." Buold opened his eyes and turned to his mate, "It begins."

Myran understood the significance of the blowing, though not the actual threat. It did not matter. A great danger was looming. She hoped her mate would guide them safely through. No matter what the menace, she would do her duty as a wife of the Head Elder, giving him whatever strength she could.

"It begins, my husband." She leaned her head upon his strong chest, and they embraced.

- - - - - - - - - - - - - -

The Tribe had gathered quickly. By the mid sunrise they all awaited Buold at the river dais. The day had changed from bright to dull. Gray clouds loomed overhead. Everyone nervously chatted with one another, each wondering what could have caused the Srñga to be blown. They had not been waiting long when from the far left side of the gathering there started a commotion. Buold had arrived and was making his way to the dais to speak. As he passed, the nearby Dwellers were asking him questions. He merely smiled and waved a hand as he kept going determinedly towards the dais. It was a difficult task as the pressure from the large gathering, narrowed his passage.

When he had arrived and stepped onto the dais a great wave of awareness to his presence was mumbled throughout the gathering. Buold raised his arms indicating that the speaking should stop and that they should all listen to what he was about to say. Quickly, silence filled the area.

"It is good to be alive, and with friends."

"And with friends," was responded by the congregation.

"With friends together, on such a sunrise." Buold had their attention.

"This early sunrise I have traveled. For some time now there has been inside a great darkness. It has troubled me. I could not understand the meaning, though I have spent much thought upon it. This early sunrise I have begun to understand. I have traveled. I have seen what is to be."

There was a muffled moan of acknowledgment from the gathering. Buold rose his hands to calm them and continued:

"At first I thought that the events of the dream were already realized, but now I believe that this has been a premonition. The darkness I have inside, is of the greatest *Evil*. The Balance of Three is threatened. To the north along the great river, many Outworlders will come. They will cut our forest and enslave those of us whom they find."

Another outcry of shock came from the gathering. Buold calmed them by raising his hands and continuing:

"I believe they will come here soon. They will dam part of the river in their search for power, then proceed here to find us. The darkness of which our recent travelers spoke (there had only been Julian, Darla, Eruinn and Thiunn) is a sign of their *Evil*. We must prepare for their arrival. We must increase our awareness of all the dark Outworlders, and divert their course. They know where were are, but we must lure them away from us. The ones of 'the City' must be found. We must help them. They are still in need and carry great Magic. I have dreamt these things. They must continue their journey before the dark ones can follow. They are our obligation and will extricate us from this *Evil*. Thodox and Quei will lead a party to find them. They must be safely guided through the forest and back to their world, while we delay the darkness. There will be great cost."

As Buold said these words slowly a hush fell upon the gathering. Each member of the tribe realized what he meant, and that there was no other option. It was their obligation to a very old promise.

"I do not know how long this will take to come to pass. We have been warned. I know it is very close. We must act soon and quickly. Each of us," Buold indicated the other Elders who were standing behind him on the dais, "will help you to prepare. Follow their words. I have instructed them each thoroughly on their duties and apportioned you all amongst them. They will call upon you now. Together we will form a union that will be impregnable."

Each of the other Elders stepped forward. They held a sheet of paper with thirty names. Buold had met with them after his alarming dream. They had been summoned early to his home before the gathering. They would organize the tribe.

"I call Quei, Thodox, Gitec and Fevol to my home. Please come directly."

Buold could not see them in the crowd. He paused and turned to the Elders and spoke words only they could hear. The rest of the tribe was swelling forth in nervous discussion. Buold turned to face the tribe to savor one last moment, before what was to follow in the sunrises ahead. He hoped they would all be safe, but knew that many of them he would never see again. With a tear in his eye, he raised his hands for silence.

"It is good to be with friends on such a sunrise. It is a good sun."

Each member knew to what Buold was referring. They intuitively understood his greeting and farewell.

"It is a good sun." was replied.

Buold turned and exited the dais. He was feeling peculiar and wanted to get back to his home and brief his two dearest friends on their mission and then rest. It would be the most dangerous journey to which he would ever have knowingly condemned anyone. He believed that the strangeness within him was a part of the orders he must give, and wanted to get it done quickly. As he left through the gathered tribe, the remaining Elders began the process of calling names and separating them into their sections. There was a great amount of distraction.

By the time Buold arrived at the trunk of his tree top home, Quei, Thodox, Gitec and Fevol had been waiting several moments. They had been near the back of the gathering and had made their way faster than Buold.

"Follow me." Buold walked past them and to the lift. His mind was elsewhere, and there was a growing turmoil within him.

They each entered. Thodox closed the door and Buold then started the lift. Not a word was said. Buold stared off into the distance as the lift rose. Thodox gave Quei an inquiring look, and both shrugged to indicate their unified surprise at Buold's preoccupation with whatever was on his mind. There was an oddness to his behavior. He felt like a stranger.

When the lift finally arrived at the top, Buold opened its door. He exited first, walking into his home and then into his meeting room. Quei, Thodox, Gitec and Fevol continued in tow.

"Close the door."

The door was closed. All four Dwellers stood tensely waiting in the middle of the room. Buold had crossed the room and was now sitting behind a beautiful wicker-like desk, facing the Dwellers. He was very stern and appeared very stressed. He directed all his attention to Quei and Thodox as he interrogated.

"You said that our visitors were safely led to an entrance?"

There was a slight hesitation, between the two

Dwellers each waiting for the other to answer. As was always the case, Quei answered:

"Yes."

"There were no problems or anything of note?"

"Well…"

"Well, what?"

"We did have a little problem when crossing the river, but it was just a minor mishap."

"Go on."

"When we came to cross, both of us had no difficulty, but the Outworlder became caught in the current and swept away. He was a poor swimmer. We thought he was lost, but he managed to get across in the end."

"I don't understand."

"Well, he was pulled deep into the current and went under. We both searched, but never found him."

"So how did you find him?"

"We didn't. He found us."

"I thought you said he was taken under by the current?"

"He was…he must have resurfaced farther down than we searched and then found his own way back to us later."

"Later? How much later?"

"It was a long time."

"Yes."

"That eve."

"Yes."

"We thought he had drowned and after not finding him, made camp. Late in the eve he appeared."

"How did he explain his appearance?"

"He didn't, and we were so overjoyed at his being safe that we never thought to ask. We assumed he had been washed away down stream and eventually got to the shore and made his way back."

There was a pause as Buold considered. He was not angry. He would have done the same thing. Quei and Thodox were nervous.

"It is very strange. How is it that you two made the crossing, yet the Outworlder was carried off by the current?"

"The current started to change just as he went into the water. It was strange. I didn't think about it, but now I remember."

"And you, Thod?"

"No, Quei is correct. At the time, we were so afraid for the Outworlder that we did not notice. If we had, I think we just thought on it as one of those unpredictable things that can happen. Thinking back, it was most unusual. The change was only in the Outworlders immediate area, nowhere else. I hadn't really noticed till your asking now."

"But how could he survive such a current if he was not a good swimmer? Surely he should have drowned?"

Thod and Quei looked to each other, Quei answered:

"We don't know."

"Odd, isn't it?"

They both answered in unison:

"Yes."

"There is something very strange about it all. I sense that it is connected with our current situation."

"We apologize for not mentioning this before, but it..." Quei spoke, but was cut off.

"There is no need. You have both acted superbly. There is much more to this than you could or should have known. It makes no difference, but the information may be of use to me. There was also the strangeness during your bringing him from the Moonfruit. Both of these occurrences are significant. I should have better prepared you."

There was a short uncomfortable pause. Buold then turned his attention to the other two younger

Dwellers who had helped to guide the female and two young ones.

"And what of you two?"

"Sir?"

"Sir?"

Was there anything unusual?"

"No."

"Well, not 'unusual', but it was 'strange' how after we all met, that the Outworlders didn't need our help. They seemed to lead us."

"Yes, you are right. I remember wondering why Fevol and I were there. They were not lost. They knew where they were. In fact they found an entry that we did not know about."

"Anything else?"

"No."

"No."

Buold turned and faced the outside. He was trying to piece all of these things together with his dream and the darkness he felt. He was also trying to understand the growing distraction within his consciousness As he searched for some meaning there came a voice. The sound seemed to emanate from the forest. It repeated two phrases:

'They must go to the Marks with the Words. There they will know all that is Old.'

Buold was awe struck by its sudden emanation,

yet instantly understood. Another secret being or wisdom inside him abruptly awoke. It was his duty to direct the Outworlders to the Marks. He knew this must be done. He knew that if they could get to the Marks before the darkness, then all would be safe.

The four Dwellers were becoming fidgety as they waited for what they believed to be, an abnormal time. Buold was in the room in front of them, but he wasn't there with them. Something was happening, but they were not appreciative of what. Finally Quei spoke:

"Sir...sir?"

This startled Buold from his thoughts and returned his focus to the immediate purpose and why these four Dwellers were standing in front of him. As he turned, their vision was drawn to Buold's eyes. They were changed from moments before. They were very glazed and larger than the usual size for a Dweller. Each of the four glanced stupefied at one another, but tried not to show this reaction to their Head Elder.

"Yes, sorry. There are many decisions to be made.' Buold had not noticed their amazement. He continued in a soft but powerful tone. His voice was also changed. It was old and of great sagacity:

"That is why the four of you are here. You are to find the Outworlders. They, we, are in great danger. They have not succeeded. I cannot tell you more. You must find the Outworlders and bring them these words."

"Sir?..." Quei questioned the orders and was about to comment on Buold's change, but was ignored.

"Go to the entry where you left the Outworlders. They will return. They are being lead back to us. Tell them they must go to the Marks with the words. There they will know all that is Old."

Buold was definitely changed. They clearly could see it in his eyes and hear it in the tone of his voice as he spoke. He gave the impression of being with them all here, but at the same time was somewhere else. He could see somewhere else. It was not a threatening change, but one of great propheticalness. He continued:

"The Outworlders go to the Marks with the Words. There they will know all that is Old. Do you all understand?"

The four Dwellers nodded yes.

"The Outworlders must go to the Marks with the words. There they will know all that is Old." Quei repeated out loud, as the others silently committed these words to memory. There would be no questioning their Head Elder. They each respected his position and wisdom.

"Then go now. You must hurry, and beware of the Gotts."

There was a moment when they all regarded one another. Thod was the first to break the moment and turn to the door. He opened it and allowed the others to leave. Before he left, he turned and faced his old friend and Head Elder.

"It is good to be with friends."

"With *friends*, on such a sunrise." Buold acknowledged through his tonality of response, the greater question being asked by Thod.

A satisfied Thodox smiled, exited and closed the door.

Chapter 6.

"How long has she been this way?"

"She was this way when I found her...I came to check. There was no answer, so I came in. I found her there...like that."

"Did you do or touch anything?"

"No. I was calling her name, but she didn't answer. I was worried. Last night she was so cheery. How could she..."

"There, there...she'll be okay."

"But didn't she..."

"No. I'm not sure what has happened. There is only one pill gone. I don't know if she took it or not, but that isn't enough to do more than just help her to sleep. If she did take the pill, it wouldn't still be strongly in her system. It would have worn off by now."

"Oh thank you."

"I haven't done a thing."

"When I saw her lying there and then the medicine on her stand, I feared that she…"

"I know. It must have been a terrible scare."

"Yes."

"You saw her here…?"

"Yes. She was happy at being home, both Andof and myself saw her safely in before we made our way home. We all had just arrived back from Pers. Lenore stayed with our family during the trouble."

"And you are certain that there was nothing out of the ordinary…?

"No. Nothing. She was happy to be home, though a little upset at being without her sons and brother. She didn't say anything, I just sensed it. We left because she seemed fine. Maybe we should have remained?"

"No. There is nothing here that you could have prevented. There is something other than medication involved, but I don't know what it is. Lenore is not drugged, and I cannot find any cause or explanation for her to be in a coma. In all my times I've seen nothing like it."

"What are you saying?"

"If I didn't know better I would say she, she is, is fighting against something. Her mind is…I don't know, but she is far away."

"I don't understand."

"Nor do I. While I was examining her she began mumbling strange words and struggling. I thought she was about to wake up, but she didn't. Then she stopped all sounds and remained still. It is as if she is caught in some bad dream, and can't let go."

"It must be a pretty vivid dream."

"Yes, I know that seems impossible, but that was how it appeared."

"Is she in any danger?"

"No, I don't believe so. There is nothing that I can find wrong with her. There is no fever, or…"

"What are we to do then. Should I, or Andof stay? How long will it be?"

"There is no knowing. It could be long or instant. There is nothing that you can do, other than watch over her. Keep her as comfortable as you can. There is no need to have both of you here at once. If it turns into a long coma, you will need to decide…"

"We will look after her no matter how long."

"Yes doctor, my wife and I will take turns if

need be."

"Well, that is truly kind of you both."

"She is like a daughter to Andof and me. She is part of our family. We could not put her in the hands of others."

"Well, I don't know what else to say. I'll stop by everyday to check. If there are any changes, please let me know immediately."

"Is there some danger?"

"No. No. I just want to be on top of this situation. You can never tell in cases like these. It's just precautionary."

"Oh." Mrs. and Mr. Reed sighed.

"Good bye then." The doctor was ready to leave.

"Let me see you out." Andof started to walk with the doctor and they both went down the hall to the main entrance. Mrs. Reed rose up after they had left and peered into Lenore's bedroom. Lenore was asleep.

"Oh Lenore. What has happened? Where are you? She moved into the room and sat on the bed near to her. She took hold of Lenore's hand.

"I am here with you. Everything will be alright. I know you can hear me. Please try to wake. Your family will be safe. Andof and I will take care of you till you decide to wake. I have your hand."

She caressed it, "If you need me call out. I am here." Mrs. Reed leaned over and gave Lenore a kiss on her forehead. Then letting go of her hand, rose and returned to the main room. As she returned, Andof had just come back.

"Oh Andof, will she be alright?"

"I'm sure she will soon awake. She'll be fine."

"So many strange things have happened this summer season."

"Yes. There is a strangeness now. I feel it."

"So it is not only me."

"You too?"

"Yes."

"I think all of this is a long way from being over. We will just have to wait and pray for the best."

"Yes. I hope her family is safe."

"She will always have us, no matter what happens."

"The daughter we never had. How unpredictable things are." Mrs. Reed smiled at her husband.

"Yes, the daughter." he smiled back.

They both stood together and watched the sleeping Lenore, wondering what could have caused her to be in such a condition and whether or not she would soon awaken. They were prepared to wait as long as it might take.

Lenore was deep within the Magic. Her consciousness was now linked through the Balance and providing support to her brother. In her conflict with the *Evil*, she had linked herself through the Balance to her brother. By calling out to him and combating the strength of that *Evil*. Lenore had instantly decided to support Julian. She had managed to distract the *Evil*, so that Julian was able to concentrate his own Magic on his purpose. The drain from Lenore had been tremendous. She was almost devoured by the darkness. She would need time to recover, to reestablish 'her-selves', while at the same time standing watch within the linking through the Balance. Every segment of her power was either used or still being used to maintain the linking. She knew Julian had heard her. Lenore understood that she had needed to distract the *Evil* by adding further drain to the Balance. It was the only way to help her family. Her fate was now intricately dependent upon the security and success of them all.

Chapter 7.

"Uncle Julian!" Eruinn excitedly shouted as he recognized the watery creature. Thiunn stood dumbfounded.

"Is that you?" Julian spurted out with difficulty as he kept his head above the water. Though disoriented from his swim, he was just as astonished as the Young Ones at being reunited.

"Over here. Come to the edge and we'll help you out." Thiunn directed. He surmised his Uncle's directional dilemma.

Through the water Julian clumsily made his way over to them. He was relying more on the sound from Eruinn, than sight. The underwater trip had irritated his eyes and they were not yet adjusted or working properly. As he came closer he noted that there were two standing on the ground ahead.

"Where's Darla?" Julian was adjusting and saw by the light of the cavern, that only his nephews were on the bank.

"She's with you." Eruinn announced as if it was a silly question for his Uncle to ask.

"Me?"

"Didn't she find you and send you in here?" Eruinn's gaze was more questioning.

"No. I haven't seen anyone since the tunnel." Julian had made it to the shallow water near the path and was now being helped out of the water by the Young Ones. He was happy to be reunited with Eruinn and Thiunn. Now he might be able to complete his task. They helped their Uncle onto the path and placed him seated upon the firm ground. They sat next to him. Eruinn continued:

"Darla left here moments ago. She was hoping to find a way out."

"I didn't see her. The passage under the water is tricky. It's hard to see in the water. Perhaps...There was something. I thought it was a creature within the water."

"Where?"

"Just near the last passage. Maybe it was

Darla."

"It was probably her. She just left here not long ago."

"On the other side of this pool through a series of passageways lies the river. She will know how to get there." Julian's assuredness came from within.

"Then she will return to us."

"Yes. There is no way along the river to travel."

"What happened to you in the tunnel? Where did you go?"

"It's a complicated story, and I'm not sure I understand it completely."

"How did you manage to survive? We thought that you would never...We thought you'd be..." Eruinn hesitated.

"Dead." Thiunn filled in the space.

"Well, after I fell into the canyon abyss, I thought that was it too, but then I found myself in a strange shaft. It was a horrible experience. Everything that was in my head was happening all at once. Any thought or image that I paid the slightest attention to became real."

"Where was this shaft?" Thiunn was now involved in the conversation. The shock of his Uncle's reappearance was now wearing.

"I don't know. I don't even know how I got into

it. The next thing I realized, I was about to fall into the river." Julian did not wish to tell everything. He minimized the events.

"It must have been the Magic." Thiunn was enthralled.

"But how did you find your way here?" Eruinn prodded.

"From inside."

"Inside?"

"When I made it to the river bank I just understood what to do. I followed the river upstream till it ended on the other side of this waterway. It is an entry to Tika from the days of the Old Ones…"

There were more questions from the nephews and Julian attempted to answer them the best way he could. He marveled at the new depth of knowing that ever since his jump into the abyss, had become a part of him.

- - - - - - - - - - - - - -

After Darla passed into the underwater passage from the deep pool leaving Eruinn and Thiunn behind on the path in the cavern, she began to feel that she had come this way before. She couldn't place when, but she knew she had, and that she must keep going to her left. To her left ran in her head. Her heart was pounding. She maintained a close distance to the left wall of the underwater passage. There was a very dim light being provided from luminescent plants that covered the submerged walls. Darla found it interesting that the same plant life of the other passageways also grew under the water.

She swam. Length after length. Soon she wondered if there really was an exit to the outside world, or if she was fooling herself. A silent knowing inside her pushed her forward. It was not long before the first rest cavern was reached. She swam up into it and kept treading water as she drew in more air. Then she submerged and made her way along, in search of the end of this system of passageways, and a way to the outside.

It was in this next passage that the light and the plants disappeared for a short stretch. Darla allowed her left shoulder to keep brushing against the wall as she swam through the pitch darkness. It was terrifying not knowing where or how long this section of the passage was going to take to swim beyond. About two lengths into this darkness, she collided with something large. She knew from the contact that it was a living creature of some sort. She panicked and swam as hard as she could to get away from it. Several lengths after the collision the plant life reappeared and there was the murky light once more. Her air supply in this section was being strained as the passage went on. Just as she expected to asphyxiate and then drown, she found the next rest cavern. Breaking through to the air she let out the agony that had been held within her since the collision. She was scared and felt vulnerable. Would the creature chase after her? She was uncomfortable remaining in this cavern very long. Very rapidly she filled her lungs with air and proceeded on her journey.

She swam harder, partially because of the fear of the return of the creature, and partially due to her desire to find the end to this 'test' of her abilities. She moved through the water sleekly. Gradually she began to feel that the water here in this section was cooler. She assumed she must be near the river. She swam harder. Her breath was becoming increasingly small. All she focused upon was keeping left within the dim murkiness of the water.

At the point where her breath expired, she forced herself beyond normal limits and found herself at the end of the passageway. She arched her head backwards and looked upward to where a mass of light was entering the water. She ascended, pulling herself up through the water. In four lengths the water became turbulent and there was a current moving her in a circular way. It became difficult to swim. She struggled against the current. She bumped and brushed against a wall. She outstretched her hands to protect herself from harm. Her hand found a ledge along the wall. She grabbed onto it and pulled herself close. She became secured. Slowly she followed the ledge and managed to progress along it. It was going up. Next she found a footing and together with her hands and feet began to scale upward. She was on some sort of natural stairway. There was no need to swim. It was not long before she had managed to walk up through the water and into the fresh air of the outside. All she could hear was the sound of the whirlpool that she found herself within. Then she was aware of another greater sound. The sound of the roaring river. She had made it.

Darla continued walking up and out of the pool, to where, unbeknownst to her, Julian had earlier entered into the same water. She stepped out of the water and collapsed onto the ground. There was a way out. She had found it. She must hurry back to Eruinn and Thiunn. They would all be on there way soon, was the first thought that entered her mind. Then her second thought was to get a good look at the location of the exit.

Darla reconnoitered. She was on the eastern side of the river. There was a pathway stretching along this side of the river off into the distance along with the flow of the powerful water. In the other direction, against the flow of the river, was a huge boulder that was forcing the water into two channels. This was the spot she had seen from the Tunnel opening above while searching for Julian. She probed into the heights of the canyon above, for the Tunnel of Light, but was not able to see it. She considered that Julian might be lying nearby after his fatal fall. Darla made a quick visual scan of the shoreline—nothing. She scrutinized the pathway that lead from the whirlpool along and down the bank. She saw the winding path and many wet spots. They followed a very regular pattern. Her subconscious analyzed this regularity. Rising up and walking away from the pool Darla started to investigate. They were foot marks! Someone had passed this way and not very long before. The marks were coming from way down the path to the whirlpool. The foot prints were small, about the size of...Julian. It was Julian.

- - - - - - - - - - - - -

"And that's about it. We have to go to the Level of the Keeper and get the *Passwords*. The *Evil* will know the *Passwords* are there. They must be taken and hidden."

"Where." Thiunn asked.

"I'm not exactly sure, but it has something to do with *Marks*."

"Marks?" Eruinn repeated.

"That's all I know. We must get them and then get out of here. I think the best way is to go back to the Burning Forest the way we came. It will be the safest course to take."

– – – – – – – – – – – – – –

Darla returned the few steps to the whirlpool and entered the water. It must be Julian. He was alive. She descended into the pool the same way that Julian had done, took a large breath and started the swim back the way she had just come. This time she would keep to the right. She was excited to get back. Inside she sensed Julian's nearness. The fear of the 'creature' of the passageway was gone. It had been Julian.

Darla swam determinedly. It did not take as long this time to swim through the passages. She was now in the last passage and approaching the cavern from where she had started. A light shone from above. Darla swam for the surface and broke through shouting:

"JULIAN!"

The noise of something breaking through the water behind Eruinn, Thiunn, and Julian startled them. For an instant there was fear, which was followed, as soon as the voice was understood, by exultation.

"Darla." Julian replied as he rose to face her soggy visage.

"I should have known that the creature in the water was you." Darla smiled as she made her way to the shore. She was helped out by all three of the Jardians, and they each in turn hugged and welcomed each other.

"I didn't think I would see you again so soon after that stupid trick of yours." Darla meant the jumping. It was done in a lighthearted manner. "What happened? How did you get here?"

"It was bizarre. One moment I was falling to my death, and next I was in this shaft."

"Shaft? With many colored particles?"

"Yes. Have you seen them?"

"No, but I have heard of them before, from others that knew of them. In my early time as…" Darla changed what she was going to say. She had already said too much. It was not her place to tell more. "They are called the Labyrinths of Light."

"Labyrinths of Light."

"Yes. They are all part of the Magic of the

Balance. It is said that the Old Ones used them to travel. I do not know where, but there is great Magic within them. Only the most pure of purpose can enter.

It seems there is more to you than we know."

"I don't know about that, but 'They' did save me. It was difficult to be there. Thought became reality. It's hard to explain."

"There are many strange occurrences since our trip began." Thiunn added, "I'm beginning to understand more about things that I have never known."

"Me too." Eruinn agreed.

"All of us. We are the Chosen." Julian stood proudly. "We are all the last of a long line of beings. We are charged to protect the Balance."

"Yes, your Uncle is correct. Now that you are each able to recall more, I can tell you that we are all of those beings, the Old Ones. We have had an ancient awakening. One that will change each of us forever. We may never be the same again. There is no returning to our old selves."

"Because of the *Evil*?" Thiunn asked, remembering his encounter in the cottage in Jard.

"Yes. Even now it searches for us. Only we stand as obstacles in its way. It wants the Magic of the *Passwords of Promise*." Darla paused and looked to Julian.

Julian without further prompting explained further,

"I know that we must hide the *Passwords*. The *Evil* has found the Key. It is almost in his grasp. Lord Merm will retrieve it from the river. It will not be long before they come for the *Passwords*. We must hurry to take them from this place."

"Lord Merm is alive?"

"Yes Thiunn."

"We have been here before, haven't we?" Eruinn was understanding.

"Yes. I hope we will not need to be here again under these conditions." Julian directed his words beyond them and toward whatever Magic was near in the caverns of Tika.

"We are all changing. We will understand better soon. Now we should continue and complete our task." Darla did not want to waste a moment. The Magic was stronger amongst them now. It would be easy for the *Evil* to track them.

"You are right. We must go to the level of the Keeper. I know the way." Julian did know the path to follow, it was deep within his shared consciousness. He turned and walked along the path to the entrance of the stairs that led up to the various levels of the city:

"This way. It is not far above."

They all followed after Julian into the stairwell. It was very brightly illuminated by the plants. Their collective Magic was gaining strength. The plants were now able to absorb greater amounts from them.

The stairwell was not large. It only allowed enough height and width for each of them to pass singularly. The stairs rose rapidly, similar to the ones in the underground passages enroute to Norkleau. They were old and carved from the rock. The walls were covered with plants. Only the stairs themselves were barren rock. There was no echo as all sounds made by their climb were consumed and muffled by the plants. There was a 'close' sensation. It was comfortable and secure.

The stairwell went straight up in a zigzag fashion. Every fifteen steps there was a small platform area and then another set of stairs rising up, zigzagging to and from as they continued upward. This went on for several sets of two, and then opened into a cavern on the first level above the river entrance. They crossed the cavern to the stairwell at the opposite side and again walked up. There was a sameness to everything.

At the seventh level Julian stopped, entered the cavern and waited for the others to gather around him in the center of the room.

"It is here. On this level. We are looking for the sign that indicates a door."

What sign?" As Thiunn spoke he knew. "Oh, the same as the other passageway doors."

"Yes. It is somewhere over there." Julian pointed and they all went to the far wall in search of the symbols that they each remembered from the Norkleau passages and the entry to the Cavern of Three.

After several moments Darla had found the symbols,

"Here they are."

Julian came to verify,

"These are them. We must each push on the symbols as before in unison."

Each stepped forward and prepared to push.

"Ready?" Julian checked with each of them.

"Ready."

"Ready"

"Ready."

"On three. One. Two...Three."

They pushed in unison. There was no tune played, just a click sounded and then the rock area that contained the symbols slid back as they pushed. The rock door stopped a length inside the wall. There was enough space to squeeze through.

Julian entered first. One by one they followed. After the last had entered, the rock door slowly slid back into place flush with the wall. It fit perfectly.

They all stood cramped together on the inside of the rock door. There was a long narrow hallway sloping upward before them. It was not illuminated, but there was a great glowing light at its far end.

"Wow. That's pretty bright." Eruinn blurted.

"The Cavern of the Keeper. Follow me." Julian did not wait for a reply. Distracted by the sight, he continued up the hallway.

"Wait up Uncle Julian!" Thiunn called, but Julian kept walking.

Darla and Eruinn shrugged and fell in line. It was a short traverse. The closer they came, the brighter the light became. It was blinding so much that they were each forced to shield their sight from its glare with their arms. They had no discomfort. It was merely too bright for their unaccustomed eyes. At the end of the hallway they each stepped carefully into a large cavern. When their eyes were used to the brightness they beheld a magnificent large room.

"The Cavern of the Keeper." Julian was in awe like the others. Each of their inner beings knew where they were.

The Cavern was carved from the solid rock. Every space on the wall contained the ancient script. There was a pedestaled central area from which the light was coming, though its source was unknown. The light was off white, with a hint of moss color. The cavern was circular and there were two entrances other than the one they all stood before. One to their left and one to their right. The walls had a series of arched niches running their circumference. They were ornately carved, and protruded slightly away from the wall. In each niche there rested an urn and on top, where a lid should have been, was a skull. All the skulls focused upon the central pedestal. The light from the pedestal gave the impression that there were eyes in the sockets of the skulls.

Julian approached the pedestal followed by the others. There was an absolute haunting silence. He stopped about a length from it. Deep within a circular light that emanated from the area, there was an imprint of a hand. He understood what must be done. The pedestaled area was the origin of the *Passwords*. From there the *Passwords* could be accessed. Julian walked up to the ball of light that rested on the pedestal and put his hand into it, in an attempt to touch the hand print which lay atop the rock pedestal. His hand disappeared. He pulled back. His hand reappeared. The others watched. Thiunn nervously commented:

"What do we do now?"

Julian concentrated on the ball of light and the imprint while searching for something, he answered:

"This will reveal the *Passwords*."

Julian focused upon the imprint within the light once more. No one spoke as he committed his whole being to his purpose. He outstretched his harm and passed his hand into the light. It disappeared, but he kept moving forward. Soon the length of his arm was gone. Julian kept his mind upon the imprint, and imagined the position of his vanished arm within the light. He saw in his mind his hand as it began to feel the imprint. His hand fit it perfectly. The others watched as Julian stood still with his arm lost inside the light. He seemed to be listening to something but they did not hear anything, but they understood. They remained silent.

"Julian, my son. Go to the Marks. The Dwellers will know."

"Yes, father." Then, there was a pause.

"Repeat the words and 'they' will be given. You must hurry."

"From all before is once more, release upon me now." Julian whispered.

There was another pause. Then a beam of light emanated from the eyes of each skull. The beams shot across the Cavern and reflected to a space to the left of the niche adjacent to where Eruinn, Thiunn and Darla stood. They ducked out of reflex, though there was no danger. Out of the spot where the collective beams had converged something began to glitter. Darla was closest and examined the phenomena. They were the symbols, but slightly different. On the one empty space within the Cavern that the wall had no designs, the symbols presented themselves out of the rock by exuding a marvelous variegated glow. The glow outlined the symbols long after the beams from the pedestal and skulls had ceased. They were not carved into the wall, but were lit by the beams and reflectively revealed.

"The symbols." Darla said to Julian.

"Quickly. We must unlock them." Julian crossed to the symbols. All four placed their hands upon the symbols.

"Now." They all pushed on Julian's verbal signal.

The glittering symbols sank into the rock wall as they pushed, followed by a seven note chime.

They let go. Then magically, a piece of the rock underneath the symbols vanished. They all peered in and saw two small red leather books. The *Passwords of Promise*. The books were still bound together as Julian had left them in the Cavern of Three.

"Hurry." Darla encouraged.

Julian glanced at the three of them, as if wanting their approval. He placed his right hand into the niche and carefully clutched the books. He pulled them out and while holding them in front of him, grinned, and then making space, placed them between his body and his shirt. They were safe.

"Okay. Let's get on our way. Over through there." Julian was in command.

"Which one?" Eruinn asked.

"To the right. That is the way that will lead us back to the canyon entrance."

This knowledge was certain and came from deep inside Julian's consciousness. They all crossed over to the right exit, and one by one left the Cavern. Julian was in the lead, Darla was last. As she turned and left the Cavern, the light from the pedestal extinguished. They were on their way. It would not take long for the *Evil* to find them once they left the zone of Tika. They knew they must hurry before it could snatch both the Key and the *Passwords* from them.

None of them spoke on the winding journey through the passages. Up and down, left and then right, they were taken. They were very tired. It had been a long time since they had last eaten or rested. The strain would overpower them if they did not take care.

The urgency of their task drove them, and by the late eve they had traveled and reached the passage that would lead down under the river to the canyon entry they had first found when they were with the Dwellers. They paused for a moment at the beginning decline, knowing well how arduous this passage and the climb to the other side was going to be. They were again using the illuminator to guide them. It was now shining much more brightly than the first time it had been used. The Chosen Ones were all now stronger in the Magic as was evidenced by its brilliance.

"Can we stop?" Thiunn was exhausted.

"Yes. I'm tired and hungry." Eruinn also could not continue.

"They're right, Julian. We have had very little food or rest. If we don't at least rest, we will become vulnerable. We should stop here and regain some strength."

"Does anyone have any food?" Julian inquired as he shone the illuminator in their direction, but there was no answer. Julian understood the silence,

"You're right. We'll stop here and rest. If we can get to the Dwellers by tomorrow eve, we will be able to eat. Can we do it, if we get rest now?"

There was a hesitation, upon the realization that they would all remain hungry until the next eve. It was difficult. It had been two sunrises since they last ate.

"We will do it." Darla spoke on behalf of them all. "I needed to lose a little weight anyway." They all chuckled at this absurdity.

Chapter 8.

It was early in the next sunrise that the four Dwellers: Quei, Thodox, Gitec and Fevol started their journey to the place where the Outworlders had previously left them and entered the canyon tunnel. There was no fanfare, the four left unnoticed. Their plan was to retrace their original route and end up at the point where they had left the Outworlders. Being veterans of the forest and not hindered by 'guests', they estimated that they would arrive at the location by after the mid sun. Quei and Thodox were the most senior and naturally took charge of the expedition. They decided that they would spend two sunrises at the canyons and then Gitec and Fevol would scout around to the Falls of Light. If there was no sign of the Outworlders by another two sunrises, they were to come back. In that eventuality they would attempt to enter the passageway that the Outworlders had gone into. Each Dweller hoped that this would not be necessary. They did not like the idea of going into the unknown underground passages that were said to riddle the area. They did not know what to expect. They hoped that Buold's dream was accurate and that the Outworlders would return of their own volition to the canyon entry.

The four rapidly made their way northward. By the mid sun they had crossed the river at the same bend where Julian had initially been swept away, and were far ahead of their schedule. They did not stop to rest, but occasionally, as they hiked, drank from the skins that they each carried. This allowed them to cover ground more quickly.

Shortly after the mid sun, they found themselves standing atop the canyon flats overlooking the entrance to the underground passage. There was no sign of life. There was nothing of the Outworlders in sight. They decided to make camp and prepared to wait.

- - - - - - - - - - - - - -

"*Julian. Julian.*" it was his father's voice.

"Yes. Father."

"Hurry. There is much danger. The Magic of the Passwords will conceal you. Read the Marks, the Marks of Stone."

"But what are they? Where do I find them?"

"Buold knows the answer. He will show you the way, but only the Chosen can protect the Balance. Read the Marks."

"Father?"

"Read the Marks. Hurry..."

Julian was startled and abruptly awakened. He had no idea of how long they had been asleep here in the passage. The illuminator was dim but cast enough light so that he could see his companions, who were asleep next to him. Julian was a little unnerved. It was time to leave. Something inside was pushing him.

"Hey. Wake up. We've rested long enough."

He leaned over and gentle roused them by shaking and calling for them to wake up. There was complaint from each as they woke.

"How long were we asleep?" Eruinn asked.

"I don't know, but we'd better get going." Julian, now standing, patted the left front of his shirt feeling for the books. They were safe.

"We should be at the entrance soon. Remember last time." Now Darla was also standing.

"Hey, Thiunn. Wake up!" Eruinn shoved his

sleeping brother. "You look like an old log."

Thiunn groaned as he slowly became conscious. "I'm hungry."

"We are all hungry. Get up. The sooner we get to the entrance, the sooner we will get to the Dwellers, and food." Julian was watching as Eruinn was prodding his brother. "All we have to do is follow this passage down and under the river, then up the other side to the entrance."

The thought of the effort that would be required to make this last leg of their journey was disheartening to the weary Southlanders, but they did not express their fatigue. They each knew from their lack of enthusiasm that they would rather not have to make this trip, but there was no choice. Reluctantly they readied themselves. The hunger was causing them to be short of temper and distracted. There was no solution to their present condition, other than completing the journey and getting to the Dwellers as soon as they could.

Julian lifted the light toward the passageway. The illuminator did not show much that he did not already know. It was just as steep and unpredictable as before. There was no point putting off commencement of this stage of their journey any longer. Julian took a deep breath, shook his head and then, remaining in the lead, started down the passageway.

- - - - - - - - - - - - - -

It was a clear and beautiful sunrise at the canyon entrance. The four Dwellers had risen early. Gitec was starting a fire. The other three were closer to the entrance and overlooking the canyons. The sight was extraordinary.

"What a fine sunrise. It is hard to believe that so much trouble is out there." Thodox made an outward motion with his left hand to emphasize his words.

"Yes. It is sad." Quei was half in thought as he spoke.

"Do you think it will be this sunrise?" Fevol questioned.

"Who knows? It could be. Buold has foreseen something. If it is not this sunrise, it will be the next, or the next, but the Outworlders will come. He has never been wrong before." Quei finished, and there was a long pause. There was no questioning of the ability of the Head Elder. His skill in the dream state was absolute.

"Fevol. You take the first watch here. Thodox and I will relieve you by mid sun."

"Uh-uh." he indicated acceptance.

"Keep an eye out. There might be others..." Quei indicated the area around and beyond,

"...looking for our friends."

"Okay."

"We're going to have a quick 'look-see'."

With that Quei and Thodox left Fevol to his duty.

- - - - -

Each step along the passageway down, had been treacherous. The air had become more and more damp, and the walls moist. The rock underneath was slippery. They used their outstretched arms to help secure their footings. It was a slow and long process, but they eventually came to the bottom. They decided not to rest, and continued on under the river. The floor of the passageway appeared wetter than their initial crossing. They wondered if the weight of the river was close to collapsing in upon them. They hurried on. Their feet becoming wet and clammy. They wanted to get out of the passage.

They were feeling uncomfortable and hungry, but there was also a worry or darkness inside them.

"Uncle Julian?" Thiunn, who was immediately behind him, asked.

"Yes."

"I'm feeling strange."

"It's the hunger."

"No. I don't mean that type of strange. I feel afraid. There is something bad happening."

"I feel it too." Julian had not mentioned this before. He thought that he was the only one sensing a darkness inside and did not wish to alarm the others. It was growing. The farther he was getting from Tika, the more he was afraid.

"Is it the *Evil*?"

"I think so. It will not be long before it is aware of us, if it isn't already. We must hurry."

"And the Key?"

"The *Evil* will soon have it. Merm will find it for him. Then 'he' will want these." Julian knew at that point the *Evil* would have such dominance over Merm that they would essentially be one together. As he spoke, he patted the books hidden under his shirt.

"We have to get the *Passwords* away from the *Evil* as fast as we can. The Dwellers can help us."

"How?"

"I don't really know. I just know that we must take the *Passwords* to the Marks of Stone."

"What are the Marks of Stone?"

"I'm not sure."

"Where are they?"

"I'm not sure, but I know the Dwellers can lead us."

"What about Merm?"

"It will not be long before the *Evil* sends him after us. That's why we must hurry. We must find these 'Marks', and protect the *Passwords,* before the *Evil* leads Merm to us."

"Oh."

There was silence. The conversation ended as Julian came to the inclining passage that led to the canyon entrance. They were across the river.

"We're almost there." Julian's thoughts went back to the efforts of the journey as he announced his find. There was encouragement in his voice,

"Here are the stairs. Be careful, they are very steep," Julian started in the upward direction.

The opening seemed smaller than they recalled. The steps were cut out of, and passed up through, the cliff. The tunnel was so narrow that each of them kept their arms out with hands running along the smooth cool rock, for support. The incline was steep. If one were to slip, they would all probably not have been able to recover. The entrance was very close now. They each remembered. The knowledge of its nearness enlivened them.

- - - - - - - - - - - - - -

Mid sun had come and gone. Quei and Thodox relieved Fevol. Gitec would relieve them in the late eve. The three had spent most of the time scouting the vicinity for anything unusual, while Fevol watched. They found nothing and Fevol saw nothing.

"Have you noticed how quiet it is?" Thodox was sitting upon the ledge of the canyon that led a few lengths below to the entrance. Quei was standing to one side.

"Yes. Something has changed."

"The whole area is absent of life. Everything is in hiding."

"Yes. I noticed that too. There is a stillness."

"Whatever is out there, it's bad."

"Remember the first Outworlder, Julian, when we were taking him to Buold?"

"Yeah?"

"Remember when he said he was being watched by something *Evil*."

"When he vanished, you mean?"

"And just before. He kept looking over his shoulder."

"Uh-uh."

"I think that is what's wrong. Everything has sensed that presence. That watching. Just like us now."

"Julian was very frightened by it."

"Yep, and so should we."

Both Dwellers thought on Quei's last words
- - - - - - - - - - - - - -

The climb was demanding. Every last bit of their strength was being used. They were tired and panting when Julian finally stopped. It was the end of the passage.

"This is it. On the other side is the way we first entered." Julian shined the light upon the rock wall that had abruptly ended his ascent. Darla, Eruinn and Thiunn gathered round. Darla had been noticeably quiet on the journey back to the entrance.

"There. There they are." Thiunn found the symbols that would open the rock door.

Without direction, they each touched a symbol and awaited Julian's command.

"One, two...three."

They all pressed in unison. The rock door scrapped against the floor as it opened inward. Beams of brilliant white outside light shot through the cracks. Slowly the door opened. They stepped back out of its way. The light was stronger and brighter. They shielded their eyes as they winced from the sudden change of dark to light. Then, once acclimatized and the door opened, they passed through the door and carefully onto the canyon wall ledge. It was still hard to see in the brightness.

- - - - - - - - - - - - -

The noise of the rock door's opening had started during the quiet after Quei's last words. It startled the two Dwellers. Quickly they identified its source. Someone was opening the door to the entrance below.

"Fevol! Gitec!" Quei called, and catching their visual attention, motioned them with the urgency of joining both he and Thodox. They ran over.

"Someone comes."

The four Dwellers prepared for whatever might exit. Slowly the door opened. There was a long time, then one, two, three, four exited. It was the Outworlders, Buold had been correct.

The Dwellers did not move to greet the Outworlders till the rock door began to close and there was a certainty that no other being accompanied them.

- - - - - - - - - - - - -

The rock door began to close, after Darla, being last, had exited the passage. She was having difficulty adjusting to the brightness. She, like the others, was pleased to be back in the outside worlds. Carefully the four stood on the ledge.

"How are we going to get up?" was asked by Eruinn.

"We'll give you a hand!" Thodox was first to greet them.

"Thod, Quei," Julian responded with a broad smile, "It is good to be with friends."

"With friends on such a sunrise."

The Dwellers were happy that Buold had been correct. The Outworlders appeared drawn and weary. They were promptly helped up from the ledge by the Dwellers and over the several lengths to the campsite. The Outworlders were visibly fatigued. Quei realized it was now too late in the sunrise to return to the forest community with them. They would wait. In the next early sunrise, after they had all been refreshed, they would return. For now, there was much to catch up on.

- - - - - - - - - - - - - -

It was the second sunrise since Buold's dream travel and the alerting of the gathered Dwellers. Much had taken place since then. Most of the community had started their various duties. There was no type of fortification being done, but rather camouflaging of the existing community. One of the seven groups of the tribe had been given this task. The group consisted of the young and very old. Another group of the tribe had been instructed and sent throughout the forest to guard and send an alert of any intrusions of any kind. Each of the seven groups of the tribe was busily seeing to its duties, here, and throughout the forest. Even the Moonfruit had been informed of the emergency.

Buold was in his tree top home, in his official room. He was worn emotionally. The darkness inside was gnawing at him. He wondered if Quei, Thodox, Fevol, and Gitec had arrived at the entrance. He felt sure that they had, but he would not be certain until the completion of their task. He had no doubt that the Outworlders would come. The dream state was never wrong. They would be brought to him.

Buold was seated at his large desk in his comfortable chair. The Srñga lay in its box in front of him on the desk. He was deep in thought. The smell of Blue Bark was in the room. He had lit two pieces to help calm him. The odor continued to relax him more and more. It had been a hard period. He closed his eyes to rest a moment. He was in need of sleep. He had not been able to get much peace since his dream travel, and the organization of the tribe. Now that the tribe was on its path and everything set in motion, he was able to stop for a moment and try to recoup. He dozed off.

As he dozed, in his half conscious state there

came a voice. Buold opened his eyes in his sleep. Before him in his room there was an image. It was very old and difficult to identify. It spoke:

"*It has been long.*"

"Who are you?"

"*We are of the Ones from before. We were the Ones that knew you then.*" The voice had many voices within it. It was not of a singular origin.

"My father's fathers?"

"*Yes. We are all the same. You carry the seed of that knowledge and that promise. It is within you. It is the Magic you hold.*"

"I know." Buold understood their meaning. He realized that he was attached to all the generations of Head Elders before him. The dream state was part of their inherited knowledge. He also understood that there was the ancient calling within. The obligation.

"*The moment has come. You must show the son of the one before, the way.*"

"But I know not where."

"*It is in the Great Hall of Aug. There are the Marks of Stone. You must show them the way. Only you can go with them.*"

"But what are they?"

"*The Stoneman will know the sign and the Chosen shall make the way.*"

"But that is in Aug, how can we get them into Aug?

"The Chosen know. You must lead them, but cannot enter. They must enter alone."

"Why not show them yourself?"

"It is the calling of the Promise. It must be fulfilled. They will need your Magic."

"My dreams?"

"They will need your power of sight. Then they will have all that they require to complete their task."

"What of this darkness I feel?"

"They are also aware of the dark. The Balance is threatened. Only the Chosen can restore it. There is no more. It must be done. You are called upon in the name of your fathers before."

The image lingered and then vanished. Buold came out of his sleep. He was in his room alone. He realized that he had fallen into a dream. He knew that he must act. It was his obligation to all those before. The puzzle was beginning to come together. All he could do now was to wait for the Outworlders to arrive.

- - - - - - - - - - - - - -

Early in the next sunrise, Quei roused everyone. The eve before, Julian, Darla, Eruinn and Thiunn had been fed and they had briefly recounted the tale of their journey from their first entering of the canyon passageway to the present. They did not reveal the intimate details of their purpose, only that they had been ambushed by the Gotts and Riders. The conversation had not lasted long, they had been too exhausted. They all had turned in as soon as it had become dark.

Now, it was another beautiful sunrise and Quei was anxious to return with them to Buold. While the Outworlders readied themselves, Fevol added wood to the campfire and prepared a hot drink. It was welcomed by the weary travelers. They felt much stronger after the food and rest of the eve before. This drink in the sunrise was received by them as a real treat.

"Do you feel up to the trip?" Thodox inquired while he stood around the fire drinking the beverage.

"Yes, thank you Thodox, and everyone. We were getting very close to our limits, but I think we will be able to keep up with you. The food and rest has restored much energy." Julian was pleasant.

"Yes, thank you. It was wise of Buold to send you." Darla was standing next to Julian and Thodox. The nephews and the other Dwellers were off a few lengths chatting.

"When should we arrive?" Darla further inquired.

"In-between the mid sun and early eve. It depends on how you feel."

"Good." both Darla and Julian responded as they sipped the drink.

"Before we go, I am to tell you that Buold has seen."

"Seen."

"Yes. He has told me to repeat this phrase. He said you will know its meaning: go to the Marks with the words. There you will know all that is Old."

"The *Marks?*" Julian queried.

"That is all he said. He said you should come to him quickly."

Julian was pensive. The mentioning of Marks had stirred something within him. He must hurry to get to Buold.

"We'd better get going then."

"Quei, everyone..." Thodox drew their attention by calling out in a loud voice, "It is time."

Everyone put their things together and moments later the party of eight commenced their return.

- - - - - - - - - - - - -

The sunrise had passed slowly. Buold had been restless and anxious to see the Outworlders, especially after the image and voicing. While waiting, he had prepared a small bag for the journey that he felt was soon to begin. He wanted to be prepared. Myran had not questioned him further after he had told her that he had been called to help the Outworlders. She understood and respected his duty as Head Elder, though she was afraid for his personal safety. It was now early eve, and she was in the food area preparing the dinner. Buold was outside on the balustrade overlooking the community as the light dimmed. He was smoking a cheroot. Whiffs of the sweet smoke found their way and mingled with the aroma of the cooking meal. Myran inhaled and enjoyed the security of the scent.

Buold felt calm as he viewed the homes around him. He wondered how this harmony would change in the coming sunrises. There was a stillness to the forest as the dusk fell. He drank it in as he puffed.

By the time his smoke was finished, Buold was interrupted by the arrival of a young Dweller on the forest floor at the lift to his home. The Dweller was summoned up and proceeded toward Buold on the balustrade. He had been sent with notification from the Dwellers who were assigned to watch at the perimeter of the community, that a party of eight was approaching. It was the Outworlders. Buold thanked and dismissed the eager Dweller who was proud to have been the bearer of such important news.

It was not long after this young Dweller had left, that a commotion began on the forest floor below. Quei and his party came into sight and were being greeted. They made their way to the lift at Buold's and entered. Buold crossed to the lift exit at the end of the balustrade. After several moments the lift arrived; the doors opened and the party stepped out.

"Sir. The Outworlders." was all that Quei said.

Buold offered his hand in friendship. First to Julian then the others.

"It is good to be with friends."

Julian was first to shake and respond. The others did the same.

"With friends."

"With friends."

"With friends."

"With friends."

"I am pleased that you have found your way here safely."

"With their help." Julian indicated the Dwellers.

"There is much we must speak about."

"Yes, but we are tired after our long ordeal. May

we do so in the sunrise?" Julian had taken command of the communication. That was fine with the others, especially Eruinn and Thiunn, both of whom had been pushed beyond all their previous limits and were asleep on their feet. Buold acknowledged.

"It can wait till the sunrise." He turned to Fevol and Gitec "Take them to quarters, and give them refreshment."

"Thank you. It is good to be here." Julian bowed and then was led off with the others.

"Quei and Thodox, please remain."

The two Dwellers nodded their understanding.

"Come with me." Buold turned and entered his home. Myran was standing in the main room. "I will not be long. There is a matter to discuss."

The three went into Buold's official room and closed the door.

- - - - - - - - - - - - - -

Julian, Eruinn, and Thiunn were placed in the same quarters, and Darla led to a separate chamber. Before they were parted they said their good eves. Each of them welcomed the opportunity to get a proper sleep in a proper bed.

Darla, who had been unusually quiet since the Cavern of the Keeper, upon seeing the soft bed in her private room, walked over and dropped herself upon it. She didn't comprehend why she was acting this way. It was unlike her. Within moments she no longer cared. She fell instantly asleep and into dream.

She began to relive all the events since the Cavern of Three. There was a profound change inside her, but she didn't understand. She was being drawn away, into the dark. She was in a passage alone, she felt the *Evil*. It was all around her. Jewel was drawn and in her hand. She was being stalked and cornered. A cold sweat was running from her brow and neck. The *Evil* wanted her. It was powerful, and she was helpless. A dark image hovered over her. She was being held. She was struggling. Her hands were pinned down. She was struggling. The dark image began to laugh a horrible laugh. She managed to break one hand free and tore at the image. She made contact with something solid. It cried out in pain and anger. Darla looked up and saw...

Darla awoke. She was panting and wet. She looked around the room. She was safe. It was just a dream. She wiped her brow and tried to settle herself. Part of her attributed the dream to all the recent events and the fatigue of the journey so far. Part of her felt the haunting of it as a premonition of things to come. There was nothing she could do. She rolled onto her side and attempted to clear the dream from her thought. Eventually she returned to sleep.

- - - - - - - - - - - - - -

In the sunrise Eruinn, Thiunn, and Darla were not disturbed. Julian had awakened before any of them and quietly left his quarters. It was mid morning. He was greeted by a Dweller who was seated outside the guest rooms. Upon seeing Julian the Dweller rose.

"I am to take you to Buold."

Julian nodded, the Dweller beckoned him forward. They walked the short distance along the linking balustrade from the guest room tree to the one that housed Buold. The Dweller knocked on the door. He was greeted by Myran.

"Well hello." she said to Julian. "It is good to see you again. My husband is in his room." she indicated the official room on the far side as she spoke.

"Thank you. It is good to see you too. May I?"

"Yes, please do. He has been waiting all the morn."

Julian entered the home and crossed to Buold's room and knocked.

"Come in Julian." came Buold's voice.

Julian opened the door and entered.

"Please join me. Sit here." Buold rose to guide Julian to his seat and also shut the door. As he returned to his chair he informed, "I hope you are hungry my wife will be bringing food."

"Thank you, yes."

"There is much that we must speak of. It is not for the ears of the others."

"Yes, I know."

- - - - - - - - - - - - - -

While Buold and Julian spoke, Darla, Eruinn, and Thiunn had risen. It was mid sun. When they were ready, they were taken across several connecting balustrades to another tree top dwelling. Here they were to be fed. This dwelling was much more open to the environment. It was nothing more than a large floor with a thatched roof protecting it from the elements. On the floor were several rows of tables and benches. It was a dining facility. Every object in the room was made of materials of the forest. There was a lovely openness and the view passed through the tree tops and on to forever.

They were seated together in the middle area where plates and cups had been placed for them.

"Did anyone see Uncle Julian?" Thiunn asked them both after it was clear that he was nowhere to be seen and that there were only three place settings.

"No. I thought you knew." Darla was back to her normal self. She did not tell them of her dream.

"Maybe he got up earlier and has eaten already." Eruinn was hungry, "Maybe he will join us soon. If he isn't here after we finish, then we can ask after him."

"He wouldn't have gone without saying good-bye, would he?" Thiunn was concerned.

"No. He is here. ...Somewhere." Darla's tone was reassuring. She knew that he was here. He could not continue the task without them. More Magic than his own was required now that the *Evil* was so strong.

"Buold said he wanted to talk. Maybe they are together." Eruinn recalled.

"That's probably it." Darla agreed. "Here comes the food."

From one side, three female Dwellers and two children were entering with large trays.

"Good sun." they each greeted their guests." You must all be very hungry."

"Yes, thank you." Eruinn replied.

The large trays were placed on the table around them.

"Please, help yourselves." one older Dweller

invited.

"Thank you." Darla smelt the deliciousness of the various foods.

The Dwellers left.

"Well, dig in." Darla was suddenly famished.

They ate ravenously. It did not matter to them whether they recognized the delicacies that had been prepared or not. It all tasted good. By the time they were full Julian appeared on the balustrade to the north.

"Uncle Julian. Where have you been? You missed all of this." Eruinn called him over. As he came over to them he answered.

"I already ate with Buold."

"So that's where you were." Thiunn was relieved that they were all together. He did not want to be separated again.

"Is everything okay? You look very serious." Darla was also pleased that Julian had not left without them.

"Yes. We leave in the sunrise."

"Where to?" Darla asked.

"Aug."

"Aug! But...that's..." Darla was alarmed.

"I know, but it is there that our journey leads."

"It will be unsafe. We were lucky last time." Darla knew inside that Julian was right but was still surprised. She never liked Aug, and her recent incarceration there, only added to her abhorrence.

"Buold has told me that what we seek is in the Great Hall of Aug. He will accompany us there. We will travel along to the Lake and then the underground passages

"The Marks of Stone?" Eruinn was trying to understand the awakening knowledge within him.

"Yes. It will be difficult, but Merm will not expect us to go there."

"But what if he tracks us?" Thiunn did not like the idea of going back there.

"It is three sunrises journey from here. If our purpose is discovered we will still have a great enough lead, provided we leave by the early sunrise. As long as we are watchful, we should be able to secretly enter through the passageway."

"But how will it help to take the *Passwords* there?" Eruinn was confused by the destination.

"I am not yet certain, but it will. Their Magic is strong. There is a reason hidden there under the very eyes of the Gotts."

"Your Uncle knows what we must do. It is a knowledge within him. I know this. It is not for us to question further. We are Chosen. We are to go with him so that he may complete his task."

"Yes, we cannot be troubled about this now. There is no choice. In the sunrise we will continue on the path that beckons. I hope it will not be too late."

Julian sat down next to them and picked at the remaining food. There was no more comment.

Chapter 9.

Merm was pleased with the speed at which this operation had been accomplished. The eastern side of the channel created by the rock island was now successfully dammed. It had all been done within the three sunrises since his jumping into the canyon abyss from the Cavern. It had been a tremendous feat. During the time Merm had returned here, to the island in the river, there had been a continuous stream of labor and materials from Norkleau and the surrounding vicinity. Merm had ordered that his Troops drive the slave labor hard. It did not matter that they were exploited and abused. They were expendable. Any who were too weak to work, or those unfortunates who became injured, were simply tossed into the river. In fact, such occasions were a bonus for the Troops; an enjoyment to break the tedium of the arduous river work. As part of their enjoyment of disposing of these injured workers, the Troopers gambled on how long it would take before a particular slave was swallowed up by the river. The Gotts had no need for the weak or injured. These poor souls were merely seen as a drain to the limited resources of food and drink that had been brought from Norkleau.

Merm was inspecting the dam from the bank. He had been informed by a Trooper that the work was completed. Before the Trooper had been dismissed, Merm had told him to summon the Commanders and have them meet him at the riverbank. By the time Merm arrived at the river's edge, the main Troop Commanders had gathered. There was a jovial mood amongst them. They were pleased with their work and the rapid completion of the blocking of the one channel. It was an incredible sight. The river was being forcibly channeled around to the other side. There was the sound of the wooden piles rubbing and squeaking against the might of the water. There were many thin leaks up and down the dam, but the vast majority of the water had been diverted. At both ends of the island the piles had effectively stopped the main flow.

Between the two ends of the island there was now an empty open area where the water had flowed, most of the river having been pumped out. There was a thick watery black silt on the bottom which was about twenty lengths deep and 'V' shaped. As Merm regarded this sight he realized that the strain on the piles was heavy. They continued to rub and squeak against the weight of the water. They would only last a short time against the river's relentless efforts to push through their blockade. Merm hoped the dam would last long enough to find the Key. There was no time to waste. They must act now.

Turning from his inspection, Merm spoke:

"Take every worker down in there," Merm showed them. "Line them up side by side and search every bit of the bed. *Every*...bit! Collect everything to within half a length deep in the bed. Commander Ziafat."

"Yes, Lord." Ziafat stood to attention.

"Set up some of the mesh we brought, and sift every load from the workers. Set up a chain of slaves, from there," Merm pointed out carefully, "...to there. There is a Key somewhere in all of that. There will be no rest till it is found, and it *will* be found."

"Yes Lord." Ziafat replied nervously.

"Yes Lord." There was a general reply together from each of the commanders after Ziafat.

"Go." Merm was abrupt. He did not have the diplomatic skill of Rmont. His missed Rmont. He had never appreciated his value till now.

The Troop Commanders bowed as they backed away in homage. Merm's orders would be obeyed to the letter. They would find the Key no matter what. None of them wished for the wrath of their Lord if he was disappointed.

Merm stood a moment watching as the Commanders returned to their groups of workers and began to organize them. There was alot of shouting and cracking of whips above the roar of the river, as they led the workers toward and into the exposed riverbed of the dammed channel. Merm was satisfied. He felt that it would not be long before the Key was his. With a smile upon his face he turned from the spectacle. He decided to retire to his tent and get some rest while he awaited the discovery of the Key.

Merm walked up the bank to the small encampment that had been erected for him. As he neared, two Troopers, who were posted as his personal guard, stood to attention. Merm paid them no attention. He walked by them and into his tent.

Inside, the tent was sparsely decorated. There was a cot, a narrow table, and two chairs. Merm lowered the flap of the tent entrance behind him, and went over to the cot. He tested its firmness with one hand, then proceeded to lay himself down. He had been through so much in the past several sunrises. He believed that the rest would do him good.

As he lay on the cot and became comfortable, Merm wondered about the thief who had fallen through the abyss and into the river after him. Had he survived like himself, or was he rotting somewhere downstream on the riverbed? There was no way of knowing, and it did not matter, now that the Key was almost in his possession. He shut his eyes.

- - - - - - - - - - - - - -

Dorluc was waiting. He was elated at the prospect of Merm's pending recovery of the Key, but was concerned over not being able to discover the whereabouts of the other thief who had fallen through the abyss with Merm. It was imperative that he begin the process of influencing Merm now. He needed Merm to continue the search for the *Passwords of Promise*. He awaited Merm to fall deeply into sleep.

Dorluc had originally assumed that the thief was dead, since when he had come back to his view screen after Merm had clearly survived the fall, the screen had failed to discover the whereabouts of the thief. This was a strange phenomenon as there should have been a residual Magic even within the dead body of the thief. The view screen should have easily found it and the thief's body. It hadn't. A long time had passed while it had searched. It still had found nothing. Not even the Chosen Ones that had been accompanying the thief could be found. This was not right. It raised Dorluc's suspicions. He had continued to direct the view screen to scan for them. There was still a substantial drain within the Magic, he sensed it, which indicated their presence, but there was no visible confirmation. Dorluc had considered what this meant. He had come to the only reasonable explanation: there was a greater Magic protecting the thieves from his view screen detection. Since the drain within the Magic, though fluctuating, was essentially the same now as it had been when he had first discovered the awakening of the Chosen Ones, that could only indicate that the same drains were present as before. He had isolated those drains: the four Southlanders, the Key, and the *Passwords of Promise*. The total drain, still being the same now, indicated that the same sources still existed. Obviously the thief was not dead, and the *Passwords* not disposed of, or secreted away. Dorluc understood that once the *Passwords* were successfully hidden, and as long as they were not exposed, that they would be shielded from discovery within the Magic of the Balance. As the drain was still strong, they obviously, were not yet hidden. He concluded that the *Passwords* were not given up, and that the thief or the others must have them. The Magic of the *Passwords* was concealing them from him. That being the case, Merm would have to be influenced rapidly to seek after the Southlanders. There was no telling where they might go, or how close they were to hiding the *Passwords*. Dorluc, through Merm, had to prevent their task from being successful.

The Key by itself did not have enough Magic to release Dorluc from 'The Land'. It was only when combined with the *Passwords* that the power of invincibility would be unlocked. Once Merm had the Key and the *Passwords*, then the process of uttering the words of invincibility would begin Dorluc's return to carnification. Through the secrets of the *Passwords*, Dorluc could access and change the fundamental threads of time, place and being. He could weave his existence within the threads of the physical universe of the Worlds. There would thereafter be no need for Merm, or *any* other. Dorluc could rule supreme.

Dorluc stood thinking of these eventualities as he watched the view screen. Soon Merm would be deep in his sleep. The view screen was making one more scan in search of the Southlanders. It flickered and jumped. It focused upon the Burning Forest, the Gott Mountains and then a sleeping Jard female. Back and forth between the three it went, but displayed no-one other than the sleeping Jardian female. Dorluc did not recognize the female. It was not the female of the Jeweled sword, but another. This female appeared to be a simple Jardian by the decoration of her bed chamber. There was no hint of whom she was, or what part she played in the disappearance of the other Southlanders.

In an effort to understand, Dorluc decided to summon Wakan. He could not afford to make any more mistakes. He needed to quickly determine the whereabouts of the Southlanders, whom he sensed had possession of the *Passwords*. If Wakan could help to identify why the screen was suddenly revealing this female as a source of drain within the Magic, then if was worth summoning him.

Dorluc closed his eyes and concentrated. He called out to Wakan. Gradually there materialized the opaque cloud in front of him above the view screen. It was like a porthole to another place. An image became visible.

"Yes. You have news?" Wakan expected that this call was to inform him of the recovery of the Key.

"No. The Key is not yet found."

"Why do you risk summoning me?"

"The Chosen Ones have disappeared from my view. They have the *Passwords*. We must locate them before they can hide them. I need your help. There is a new source of drain within the Magic." Dorluc indicated the female on the view screen, "I do not understand why she is suddenly appearing."

Wakan observed the display of the female. It was the one that had stopped him from destroying the thief as he had fallen into the abyss.

"She is the one who stopped us."

"Stopped us?"

"From obtaining the Key from the one that fell into the abyss. She has the same Magic as the thief."

"How do you know of her and not I?"

"She was the source of the sudden drain in the Cavern of Three and Tunnel of Light. She interfered with me. That is what led to the falling of the Gott and thief." Wakan was thinking quickly. He had not mentioned these details before. This would convince Dorluc that the fall had not been Wakan's attempt to keep the Key from him, but that this female had caused all the events that had followed.

"You never spoke of her?"

"I thought she had been destroyed. I did not expect you to believe."

"Why is she shown here?"

"I do not know. I am surprised she is living after the battle we fought. She called out the words of Old. Perhaps she has transferred her strength to the others. Perhaps that is the reason they have disappeared. Her Magic is being used to shield them from your screen."

"Yes, that could be it. She is a strong source of drain."

"That must be it. I can talk no longer. Inform me when you have the Key and know the location of the Words."

"Yes."

The image faded and the cloud dispersed. Dorluc was pleased with his decision to call forth

Wakan. It had been useful information. It went a little way to explain Wakan's intrusion in the Tunnel of Light. Perhaps it was an accident that Merm had not stopped in time at the opening into the abyss. Dorluc did not entirely believe this, but it was a possibility that he was now forced to consider. The fact that the view screen was unable to locate the Chosen Ones, because of a blocking or diffusion of the drain within the Magic by this female, was possible. Certainly there was something affecting it. It was not the Old Ones, for they would have revealed themselves directly to him, and dealt swiftly with him. It had to be caused by the unpredictable awakening of the various moles that had been propitiously scattered throughout the worlds to protect the Balance.

Dorluc again directed the view screen to the sleeping Merm. He would begin his influence and set Merm upon the trail of the Southlanders. The Key, once in his control, could be used to point the way. This much Dorluc remembered from the ages. The Key had a notch on one side where it could be placed upon any object that could act as a spindle. Thus suspended in the air the Key would find and point in the direction of the *Passwords*. It was like a compass honing to the north position. Merm would be able to use the

Key as a compass leading him to the Southlanders. Once the *Passwords* were hidden, this Magic would not work. The Key would not reveal their location. Only as long as the *Passwords* were not concealed would the Key act as a guide. Merm needed to find the Key and swiftly use it to discover the whereabouts of the *Passwords*. Dorluc felt that urgency. He closed his eyes and slowly sank into Merm's sleeping consciousness. It was an easy procedure now that Merm had accepted his image in his dreams as an ally. Merm's mind was open and receptive as Dorluc entered.

"You have done well." Dorluc began, "Soon you will be master of great power. All others will cower in your presence."

"Yes. It is almost mine."

"But there is one who has greater power. One who has fooled the great Lord of the Gotts."

"Who?'

"The thief. The Southlanders. The Key is merely a small part of the Magic. There are books of words which it will unlock. The beholder of these books is truly invincible."

"Where are these books?"

"The thief has them."

"Then I will find the thief, and get these books."

"Yes, but there is not much time. The thief will hide them. Once he has done that, only he will know their power."

"How much time?"

"It is uncertain."

"Once the Key is mine I will find the thief."

"You will need the Key to find him."

"How?"

"The Key will show you his location. Follow it like a compass. Before the books are hidden, it will guide you to them. I will do what I can, but it will not be much."

"Thank you."

"Send out Troops to the Dwellers in the forest. They will try to help the thief. Take a small troop with you to follow after the thief. You will travel faster and he is no match yet for the Lord with the Key."

"He is no match."

"I am near if you have need of me." Dorluc began to fade out of Merm's mind.

"He is no match..." Merm repeated in his drowsy way as Dorluc left. The influencing was over. He returned to peaceful sleep.

- - - - - - - - - - - - - -

The Slaves were searching the riverbed as Merm slept. Load by load of the slimy silt was dug out and sifted. Other than the normal debris, they had found nothing of importance. They had progressed two thirds of the length through this section of the river bed. It was approaching the late sun.

Commander Ziafat was becoming worried. The Lord would be very angry if the Key was not found, and he would most probably be blamed and made an example of, along with several slaves. He scrutinized the sifting as he considered his fate. Load after load passed through the mesh. It was hard to concentrate. His mind wandered and there were many false alarms.

During one moment of drifting, his eye caught a flicker of something small. It was not of stone. It was metal. He was prepared for another false alert as he pushed aside the four slaves that were sifting. He threw his hand into the silt and grasped hold of the object. It was solid. He brought it in front of him and brushed away the slime. It was a brass colored Key with an ornately carved head. Ziafat instantly knew that this was for what his Lord searched. With the eyes of the slaves upon him, he turned and hurried off to Lord Merm's tent. He made no commotion, just in case he was wrong. He did not wish to be made the fool in front of the slaves and Troop.

From within his sleep, Merm heard a noise.

"My Lord? My Lord?" Ziafat rustled the flap as he gently called. The guards had told him that the Lord was asleep. Ziafat ignored their warning. He had news that the Lord would welcome. "My Lord?" He pulled at the flap.

"Who's there!"

"Commander Ziafat, my Lord."

"What is it?"

"I have it, my Lord."

Merm jumped up from his cot and rushed to the tent door. He threw the flap open and ushered the Commander in.

"The Key?" Merm asked once they were concealed within the tent. "A brass Key?"

"Here it is, my Lord. It was found just moments ago." Ziafat displayed the Key.

Merm was elated. Finally he had recovered the Key. Now he could begin to…no, he thought. Now I must find the books. He remembered the dream. He wanted complete power. He needed the books.

"Commander, prepare your Troop. You will come with me. Also, order the slaves back to Norkleau and send the remaining Troops into the Forest after the Dwellers. I will give you a map. They are to destroy everything they find. There are to be no beings left alive. Understand?"

"Yes my Lord."

"You have earned much honor." Merm meant by the discovery of the Key. "Now we must find a thief."

"Thief, my Lord?"

"Never mind. See that my orders are followed immediately, and then return here. We will leave before the end of the sunrise."

"Yes my Lord." Ziafat bowed and exited.

Merm was engrossed with the Key. It was his again. He walked over to the table and drew his dagger from inside his left boot. It was a small blade for a Gott, very slender, and pointed at the blade end as well as the handle. He stuck it into the table. It stood erect. Sitting down on the chair that was in front of the table, Merm carefully placed the Key upon the point of the handle. It fit well. The Key floated precariously back and forth, but was balanced. As it became level, it also began to pivot. The stem began to favor a direction. It moved past and back until it became steady and pointing. Curious as to the direction, Merm took his compass from his belt pouch and held it beside the suspended Key. The needle found its normal position. He compared it to the Key's pointing. South South West. That was the direction of the lower Burning Forest and the Lake of Choices. That was the current location of the thief and the books. Merm smirked:

"I have you again."

- - - - - - - - - - - - - -

They had left early in the sunrise, before any other Dwellers had risen. Buold was determined to reach the lower forest near the Lake by late sun. There were five of them. They hurriedly worked their way over the same paths to the Moonfruit, though Julian, Darla, Eruinn and Thiunn did not recollect traversing these paths before. There was no conversation, just the crossing through the forest.

By the end of the sun, the travelers were well into the lower forest and amongst the Moonfruit Pine. At this point Julian again became aware of a presence. It was Fon.

"Welcome. There is no danger here. Come rest at my wood."

"Thank you, we will." Julian next spoke out to Buold who was leading the party:

"Are we near the great Moonfruit?"

"Fon?"

"Yes."

"It is over that way."

"I have communed with Fon. It has asked us to

camp at its wood."

"That will be a fine place to rest for the eve. We will be there shortly." Buold was thoughtful.

- - - - - - - - - - - - - -

"Where are you going? Why the lower Burning Forest? It cannot be there that your destination lies. No matter, we will be upon you soon."

Merm was thinking out loud to himself. He was trying to understand why the thief had gone in that direction. He removed the Key from its perch and placed it on a chain around his neck. He would be very careful not to lose it a second time. He then pulled the dagger out from the table and put it back into its boot sheath. He folded all the papers on the desk and packed them away. These he would take with him. He called out to his guards. They both stepped through the tent flap and saluted.

"Yes my Lord."

"Take these and bring my mount. Quickly!"

"Yes Lord." One took the bag of papers and left.

"You."

"Lord?"

"Take this, and come with me."

- - - - - - - - - - - - - -

They had made camp and were now sitting around a small smokeless fire.

"Fon is pleased to have us all in the wood." Julian was negotiating the communication between them and the Moonfruit. Buold could commune but he was not as fluent as Julian. For Buold, as with the other Chosen Ones, it also required that he was in constant contact with Fon's bark. As a result, it was easier to allow Julian to assume the role of interpreter.

"And we are pleased to be in 'its' hospitality. The Moonfruit are highly regarded by the Dwellers." There was a shuffling of branches as old and young Moonfruit responded to Buold's compliment. It sounded like a wave of applause.

"Uncle Julian," Eruinn was playing with a stick in the fire, "How do you do that?"

"The communing?"

"Yes. Why can't we?" he meant Thiunn and Darla.

"I don't know. I suppose it is my special gift. You can commune, but not as easily as me. Maybe you will be able to one day."

"We each have our gifts," Darla interjected, "I have Jewel and my talents. You have yours. Each of our separate talents are unique and special. They are gifts from the Magic. In time yours will appear."

"I hope they come soon."

"We should sleep now," Buold was enjoying the camaraderie and the adventure of the outdoors, but they would all need their strength over the next while. It had been a long time since he had gone on excursions beyond the community. It reminded him of his younger times. "We have a long way to go in the sunrise."

"Should we keep watch?" Thiunn asked.

"No, Fon says it will look after us while we sleep." Julian responded. Fon was instantly hearing through Julian what was being said, and had told him that the Moonfruit would be better equipped to keep watch throughout the entire forest, and not just this section. Julian did not explain all these thoughts. It was not necessary.

"It is right. The Moonfruit have long been the protectors of the forest." Buold added.

They each found comfortable places and lay down to sleep after saying their good eves.

- - - - - - - - - - - - - -

Merm's contingent had left at the appointed time. They were twenty in number. They would travel through the night in order to reach the lower Burning Forest. They had traveled beyond the canyons and crossed the river at a shallow position that had been found on the way from Norkleau with all the slaves and supplies. Many of the Troopers were not pleased to enter the Burning Forest.

This journey was taking them along the eastern edge of the Burning Forest along the smaller length of the Pass River and cutting along the north west edge of the Marshlands. From the Marshlands they would cut through the north eastern part of the Forest toward the most easterly part of the Lake of Choices, and then go straight down to the lower forest. This part of the Burning Forest was known to the Gotts, though seldom traveled. There was a path that led from the western border of the Gottland with the Burning Forest, down along the western side of the Lake through the forest. It led to the Southlands, though it was not the preferred route of the majority of Gotts, it was the fastest way to the Southlands from Norkleau and all points west. It was a treacherous route, and never did any Gott stop to rest till they had passed along it and into the Southlands. Colleg's tavern was the usual resting place.

Merm was heading for Colleg's. It was just below the Burning Forest to the west of the Lake of Choices. If the thief was in the lower forest, sooner or later he would be forced to stop at Colleg's. There was nowhere else in the vicinity to get supplies.

As Merm's Troop had entered the northern edge of the Forest, they had been quickly sighted by the Dwellers. Messages were sent up and down to the community to prepare against these hideous invaders. But the Gott invaders did not move toward their community. They kept to the eastern edge of the forest and were moving south. They seemed interested only in passing through and not in the pillaging of the Dwellers of the forest. They soon seemed more of a scouting, than invasion party. All along their journey they were watched, and left alone until their purpose could be clearly determined.

By the darkest moments of the sunrise, Merm had traveled far. He and his Troop had begun to enter the area of the Moonfruit Pine. Twice on the journey they had paused while Merm checked with the Key on the directional location of the thief. It was always the same as the first finding — ahead.

Merm believed that the thief would be camped for the eve. The thief would have no reason to suspect that he was being tracked. The element of surprise was still held by Merm. He drove the Troop hard, knowing how easily things could change. Merm wanted to get as near to the thief as possible before the thief was alerted to his pursuit. Once that occurred, the thief would be difficult to find. Till then, he would not be concerned about leaving clues as to his whereabouts. Merm was in his element. He was an excellent tracker.

The Moonfruit were excellent watchers. Merm and his Troop were detected as they approached the outlying area of the forest that led to their wood. Alert was communed. Fon cautiously waited to discover the purpose and route of these creatures.

Length by length, the Troop came closer and directly toward where the 'one from before' slept. It would not be long before the Troop was near and then would easily track their exact location. Fon ordered the Moonfruit to slow the Troop. 'It', Fon, was not certain if 'it' would be able to stop such a large number without affecting those beneath 'its' own branches. Fon decided to awaken the Outworlders and help them to escape before it was too late.

"Awake! They come." Fon communed with Julian's sleeping mind. "Awake!"

Julian moaned and awoke.

"They come. Many from the North."

"Who?"

"The ugly hairy ones."

"Gotts"

"Yes. They come this way. You must leave before they find you. We will try to slow them, but it might also slow you. Wake the others and go. We will try our best."

"Thank you Fon."

Julian quickly roused the others.

"It's the Gotts. They are on to us. Hurry."

Everyone jumped up, while Julian kicked dirt over the smoldering fire. In moments they were ready. With Buold in the lead they left on the path that would take them out of the Burning Forest and onto the Northern pathways along the south shore of the Lake of Choices.

"Farewell friend." Julian communed their good-byes.

"Farewell, 'one from before'."

- - - - - - - - - - - - - -

The Troop was close. There was only one major path that led along through the lower forest to the border with the Southlands. It was the most direct route out of the forest. Merm was confident that he would discover some trace of the thief soon. The Moonfruit were trying to slow these intruders, but there were too many of them to properly affect. The Troopers were riding fast and were very strong. They would require greater efforts by the Moonfruit to be stopped. Until the Southlanders were out of the Pine, the Moonfruit could not attempt further activity without affecting the Outworlders also. The Troops were too near to them.

As they rode, Merm had commanded the Troopers all to look for any trace of the thief. They slowed their pace and carefully examined the path as they rode. It was a tedious process. By the breaking of first light of the sunrise, they came to a joining of their path from the western level of the Lake to another path that appeared to come from farther Northwest and within the forest. Merm stopped the Troop and then dismounted. He made them all stay behind as he checked the adjoining path. He did not trust any other to track as well as himself. After several moments he spoke:

"There. Some have come this way within the last sunrise. There are five sets of prints. They lead off down our path. We are close. Be careful and keep your senses alert. We don't want to let them know we're on to them."

Merm remounted his steed and at a walk followed the prints. It was a long trail. The prints led Merm on and on, well into the lower forest and the Moonfruit Pine. His Troop was tiring. It was the effect of the Pine, but the fear by the Troopers of their Lord Merm rose them above the Moonfruit's breeze. They continued on.

The prints finally left the path. Merm dismounted. He could not see where they had gone. As he surveyed the area he noticed the smell of a fire. It was coming from the west about one hundred lengths away.

"Over there. Everyone down." he spoke quietly so as to be only heard by his Troop.

They all dismounted and fanned out. Merm indicated that they should approach till the fire was in sight. They could then surround the thief and his companions.

They moved through the Pine toward the fire smell. After fifty or so lengths, there was a slight knoll with a very grand Pine upon it. Merm could see the finest line of smoke rising from a spot just near the great tree. That was the spot, but he could see no-one near.

They all continued closer. It was not till they were upon the spot, that they realized that whoever had been camped here, had left, and not long ago. Merm was pleased to have found the site, but displeased at not finding the thieves. He stood at the fire examining it closely. It had been recently kicked out.

"They know we follow. He spoke out load to himself and an aide that was standing by him.

"How, my Lord?"

"I don't know, but they do. They are not far ahead. We will spred out and find their trail. It will be easier to track them now that it is light."

Fon had been watching as these Gotts searched for signs of the Outworlders. It awaited word from the Pine along the southern border that the Ones from before had left the forest. It was at about this time of Merm's discovery, that the message of the leaving was communed. Upon hearing the news, Fon ordered the Pine to use its strongest breeze. Slowly it was released upon those in the Pine. It would delay the Gotts half a sunrise and that was the best Fon could do.

Before Merm could rally his Troop together and continue after the thief, they were all succumbing to the effect of the Moonfruit. Under the temporary spell of the Moonfruit, one by one they lost consciousness, dropping to the ground wherever they were. They slept. It had almost depleted the Pine, but it had worked. Fon hoped that this short delay would be of help.

- - - - - - - - - - - - - -

Though the warning had been brief, it had been enough to allow Buold the time to lead the party

well away from the camp. They had not stopped
running until they were out of the forest and on
the path along the Lake. It was now sunrise. The
warning had come in the dark hours before the
morn. Buold sensed that they should be safe on
this path, as the Jard Guard now patrolled it regu-
larly. The Gotts would not try anything in their
presence. Especially this soon after the recent
invasion of this very area. Any Gott Troops in the
area would be carefully scrutinized. They were
allowed to travel the path, but would be stopped
and given an escort by the guard to their destination. Usually this was to Colleg's, but on occasion
some were merely traversing from the forest to
Aug. In that case, the Guard would escort them to
the foothills of the Gott Mountains and the path
that led to Aug.

By the end of the sunrise Buold, Julian, Darla,
Eruinn and Thiunn would be at the Southeast corner of the Lake, at the foothills to the Gott
Mountains. It was here that they would enter the
secret passageway that they, except Buold, had
used once before; the passageway to Norkleau
and Aug. The circle was almost complete. Being
in the Southland, they slowed their pace. Darla
noted how the pathway was more populated than
when she first had traveled it on the way to the

Jard Summer Festival. It seemed like yesterday.

The five did not interact with any but kept to their course. By mid sun they encountered a patrol of Jard Guard. Julian stopped as the others slowly continued along. He hailed the patrol leader.

"Good sun." the Leader said as he stopped.

"Good sun. We have come from the border of the forest. There are some Gotts there. They are coming this way."

"What do they want?"

"I did not ask. I just thought to mention it as you are going in that direction. You can never trust those animals. I just wanted to warn you, just in case."

"Thank you, traveler. We appreciate knowing beforehand. You are right, they are not to be trusted. We will go and find them and see what they want. We never like to be surprised by them. Thank you."

"You're welcome."

The patrol went on. Julian watched for a moment and then hurried to catch up with the others.

"That was a good idea." Darla complimented Julian.

"It will give us more time."

They kept a strong pace for most of the sunrise, only stopping briefly to drink and eat. By the late sun they had traveled along the southern shore of the Lake and were at the point where the secret passage entrance lay. Thiunn and Darla remembered the past occurrences here, well.

"This is where I got hit by the cross arrow." Thiunn was showing Julian, Eruinn and Buold. He retold the adventure with pride, though at the time he was horrified. While he did so, Darla found the lever for the entrance and opened the door to the secret passage.

"We can rest in here, inside. Come on. Finish the story in here. We don't want a repeat of those events." Thiunn understood what Darla meant. The Gotts may be near.

They all crossed over and entered through the rock door and into the passageway. Darla closed the door. Now for the first time in many sunrises she felt safe. They all felt safe. Julian pulled out the illuminator. The light revealed the marvelous entrance way as the time before. Julian and Eruinn felt they were reliving the past, but Buold, Eruinn and Darla were intrigued. Its walls and ceiling were carved with ornate pictures. Every now and again script was below one. It was the language of the Old Ones, it felt familiar. The pictures were telling a story and despite the sandy gray sameness of the rock carving, the pictures were full of life and color. In each, there was the symbol at the bottom right corner ...****...a symbol that was still unknown to them.

Looking farther along, the path went off to the right and beyond was the dark round opening. Julian, as before, took the light:

"This way. That dark area is the direction we travel. Come."

As they walked, the yellowish circle of light was thrown by the illuminator, all around. Long shadows were propelled at differing angles as Julian's motion swayed the light. It was eerie, and silent. They could clearly hear the crunching of the sandy soil under the weight of their boots.

Reaching the round darkened area, the lamp light stretched on. It revealed the corridor or tunnel. It seemed to be long. On they went as before.

The corridor ran a slight downward grade, twisted left once and then continued level. The decor was plain. There was no end in sight. They kept walking, and walking. After what felt a very long time, Julian stopped. It was déjà vu.

"Let's rest here," he suggested, "We have made good time".

There was no disagreement by the party. It had

been a long sunrise. Placing the illuminator on the flat floor they sat down. Though many uncertainties ran through their minds, they each refused to show it. They would enjoy this brief rest.

Shortly they rose and pressed onward. The corridor went on and soon narrowed. It also began to climb at an incredible rate, causing them to get out of breath by the effort of the hike.

"It won't last long. Don't give up," encouraged Julian. He remembered the first time he and Eruinn had encountered this change. Just as rapidly as the passageway had climbed and narrowed it abruptly ended. They found themselves inside the first cavernous room, which contained similar ornateness as the room of their entrance to this passageway, by the Lake.

On the other side of this cavern was the continuation of the passageway. Again they entered through the darkened tunnel to find much the same sort of climbs and falls and turns as before.

Ten times the cavernous rooms appeared, identical to the previous ones. Ten times the tunnels continued. They were extremely worn. The sameness of their journey became broken as gradually the sound of water echoed throughout their current passageway. Like the sound you hear when holding a lake shell to your ear. The illuminator was shining strongly. The passageway began to widen into another cavernous opening. Here was the big plain room containing two possible exits, not counting the entrance they entered from. They continued on with Julian and Eruinn in the lead, Darla following last.

Just like their first journey through this passageway, again time began to lose all meaning. How long they were in the passageway was unknown to them. Had it been a few hours or more? Disorientation had begun to set in upon them, coupled with their progressing exhaustion.

The water sound soon revealed the cool underground river that trailed along with their pathway. They had gone as far as they could for a sunrise. Julian noticed and spoke:

"We will stop here awhile. We have pushed ourselves beyond our limits."

Gladly they all found places to rest and without any conversation one by one fell to sleep.

In the blink of an eye, time passed. They awakened. It seemed to each of the weary party that they had just arrived a moment ago and had just heard Julian's suggestion to stop and rest. They felt cheated and disoriented.

'Surely they had only just arrived and sat down to rest?' they each silently wondered, but they hadn't.

They had been so tired that they each had fallen deeply and quickly into a sound sleep, unaware of passage of time, and now it was time to move. They did not question as they roused and started back upon their journey.

Much of the earlier sameness of the passageway continued. They walked on, and after awhile noticed a quieting of the river that had kept them company. It gradually widened and then ended. It didn't just stop, it suddenly pooled into a small pond and that was all. There must have been an underwater outlet, for the rate of the traveling water hadn't slowed. There was a chill in the corridor, causing them to have goose bumps. On they went for a few hundred lengths then as expected, the passage, which had been level for the longest time, turned sharply to incline. It wasn't long before the five were climbing a steep grade on hand and foot. It was most difficult.

After what seemed a thousand paces, they stood upon a plateau. It had been a long haul. The air was musty and the surfaces around them made them feel cool. They rested a moment, recuperating from the climb and looking, as far as the light permitted. There ahead, was the other final stairway. It was beautifully carved out of the rock. They began to climb.

"This is it." Julian announced.

"Look. Up there to the right. There is the narrow beam of light. There, do you see it? Just to the right …ahead, about seventy lengths," Eruinn was pleased to find the landmark.

"Aug. This is the way to Aug." Darla felt a chill as she recalled her imprisonment.

"Do not worry. All will be well." Buold placed a hand upon her shoulder.

- - - - - - - - - - - - - -

They had lost valuable time. Merm had been the first to awaken. Dorluc had helped. Upon his falling to the ground Merm called out in his thoughts for his ally to help. Dorluc heard the cry and immediately focused the view screen on to its source. Rapidly the view screen had found Merm and had shown he and his Troop asleep in the lower Burning Forest. Dorluc understood what had happened. He could not allow the Magic of the Moonfruit to delay his agents. Dorluc sank into Merm's thoughts. He had shouted and shouted till finally he was forced to give him a jolt of his Magic. As a result, Merm was slowly coming to.

Upon Merm's arousal Dorluc had broken his influence over Merm, leaving only the sense of urgency to follow and find the books. Merm shook his head and on seeing his drugged Troop, rose and started the process to awaken them. It had taken time, but they all awoke. Merm pulled out the Key and checked the location of the thieves. It was now almost due east. That meant they were traveling along the south shore of the Lake.

The Troop was finally ready. It was the mid sun. With Merm in the lead they galloped off down the path and through the Pine. They were headed for the Northern pathway. Merm wanted to make up as much time as he could.

They rode hard. But by the time they had made it to the border with the Southlands it was in the middle of the afternoon. As they approached, Merm noted a small contingent of Jard Guard ahead. It was a patrol. They were blocking the path. Merm pulled back on his reigns and slowed the whole Troop. As they walked Merm passed the word:

"Say nothing. I will talk."

When they were within earshot of the Guard, one of the Jardians called out. It must have been the leader of the patrol:

"Good sun. What brings you to the South?"

Merm replied as he came up to the blocked path. It was a small contingent, but he did not want to cause trouble or be identified. He covered his rank markings.

"Good sun."

"What brings you to the South?" repeated the patrol leader nervously. He was young and not experienced with the Gotts.

Merm quickly thought and then:

"We are enroute to Aug."

"Why not take the route through the Gottlands?"

"We became lost in the forest and found our way here. We know the way to Aug from here."

The patrol leader was suspicious,

"We will accompany you to the path to Aug."

"There is no need. We do not wish to take you from your duties."

"Those are our duties."

Merm realized that the patrol leader was adamant,

"Very well. We would not want to become lost again."

"No, you wouldn't." The patrol leader and Merm's stare caught each other and clearly communicated a much more threatening language.

"We must arrive quickly. I hope our pace will not be too difficult for the Guard to follow."

"Not at all. We are ready for such challenges." The patrol leader turned his mount and shouted. He broke off into a gallop.

Merm turned and smiled to his Troop and then the remaining Guard.

"After you." one Guard invited Merm and his Troop.

"Ha!" Merm exclaimed as he roughly turned his mount. He and his Troop broke after the patrol leader. The Guard fell in behind.

The ride was hard, but neither side complained or stopped. It was a challenge, a race. The travelers they passed along the route were pushed to the side by the horses thunderous approach. These travelers stopped and glared, allowing the Gotts and Guard to storm by. It was a frightening sight for the average traveler.

When the sun had set, both Gotts and Guard had reached the eastern shores of the Lake, and the path to Aug. It was an exhausting tie.

"The path to Aug." the patrol leader smugly proclaimed as Merm slowed and stopped. He had gotten there before him. It was a slap in the face of the Gott.

"Thank you." Merm begrudgingly barked.

Nothing more was said. Merm directed his Troop as it arrived to go up the path. He followed after the last Trooper had passed, never looking back.

The Jard Guard sat on their panting mounts with smirks on their faces, until the Gotts were out of sight. Then they slowly turned and painfully started their way back to where they were originally going: Colleg's Tavern. It was going to be an excruciating ride.

As soon as the Guard was out of sight. Merm called for the Troop to halt. He dismounted and set up the Key to find the location of the thieves. He was concerned that they would by now be far away in the South. The Key twisted and gradually pointed in their direction: Northwest.

"Northwest?" Merm mumbled to himself confused. He had expected the thieves to be far away to the South, not here, going to the Gottlands. "But... Aug is the only place northwest. Why would they go there?"

He did not understand why they were all heading in the same direction, but they were. If the Troop traveled well, they would be in Aug by sunrise. Merm saw his opportunity. They must ride to Aug. He was not sure how many would make it. It would be beyond the normal abilities of their mounts. These horses were already worn by the hard pace set from the Burning Forest. He saw no alternative. If he were to wait till they were all rested and capable of making the journey, he would certainly lose his chance of capturing the thieves and obtaining the power of the books. He had to go on, even if he was the only Gott to get there. There was no choice. Some would make it. He would make it. Merm called out to his Troopers who were beginning to make themselves comfortable, anticipating that they would stop here for the eve.

"Mount up. We go to Aug."

There was no sound or complaint from the startled Troopers. All were acutely aware of how close they were to the limits of their mounts.

Chapter 10.

The fifth and sixth group of the Dwellers together, numbered only forty. They were assigned along the northern limits of the Burning Forest and the Pass River. Their job was to look for and alert the forest community of any outside entry into the Burning Forest. Buold had been adamant in his direction of the other Elders, that an invasion would come from the North. It was just a matter of when, and in what numbers. He was not certain as to who the invaders might be, but assumed from his dream travel, that it most probably would include the Gotts. The Gotts were a rough adversary. Buold knew that the only hope the Dwellers might have was in being prepared and forewarned. This was the responsibility of the two advance groups. Once any intrusion into the Forest was observed, then the groups had very specific orders to follow.

It was during the darkest moments of the morn, that the discovery and watching of Merm's party was made. The two groups, now alerted, made tighter their scouting network, focusing their energies upon the area where Merm's Troop had crossed the river and entered the forest. They were watched and followed, but nothing else was done after it was determined that these Gotts were not invading, but enroute from one end of the Burning Forest to the other.

It was later, in the early morn of that same sunrise, that a second group of Gotts crossed the river. This group was quite different from the first. These Gotts were heavily armed, and about sixty in number. They were proceeding along, making a great deal of noise. It was as if they did not care if they were discovered. They were rough and clumsy in their crossing of the river and destructive of any elements of the forest that they encountered in their path.

The Dwellers of the fifth and sixth group had remained hidden within the forest as they watched. It was not their way to directly confront invaders. Once this Gott Troop's destination was clear, the Dwellers would act stealthily in their own unique way. If these Gotts started toward their inner forest community, then the Dwellers would secretly pick them off one by one, until their numbers were completely diminished. Otherwise they would be left to continue on their way. The less contact that was made with Outworlders, the better.

Quei and Thodox had been put in charge, respectively, of the two groups. They had much experience in handling intruders. Upon the sighting of this second contingent of Gotts entering the forest, they had instructed their groups to keep out of view along the path, unseen and blended as a part of the forest. Quei was worried lest these Gotts discover the 'community'. It would be impossible to fight these brutes off directly. They were too strong and large for the Dwellers. Fighting these dirty creatures would be difficult. The best defense was to remain out of sight, and in a clandestine manner, if necessitated, gradually eliminate the Gotts. He hoped, however, that these Troopers were following after the earlier ones.

The Dwellers watched as the Gotts were slowly making their way through the river and into the north part of the forest. It soon became evident that they were not following the same path as Merm's earlier Troop. This Troop was fanning out and slowly making its way in the direction of the inner community of the Dwellers. The Troop was well prepared and organized. They seemed to know exactly which way to go. They were also shouting in such a way that it was obvious they were trying to scare any unseen inhabitants of the forest along their path, back away from their advancing position. Amongst their armaments, they each carried long torch sticks, which were set aflame once the Troop was five or six hundred lengths inside the wood. As they marched they began to set ablaze the forest around them. The smaller trees and dry wood, instantly caught. The noise of the cracklings grew. It was a terrifying sight. The wind started blowing the smoke from the burning, southwestward. These Gotts were going to either flush out any living creatures within the forest or burn them alive. They marched determinedly in the direction of the community. By sunset they would arrive if they were not stopped.

Following and watching this activity, Quei and Thodox quickly found each other amongst the tree trunks to discuss their strategy. They stooped concealed, on the eastern flank of the Gotts, about twenty-five lengths to the side behind a large trunk. They were each out of breath from their exertion to find one another.

"I don't like it." Thodox started. "They know the way."

"You're right. They are headed to the community, and will burn us all out."

"What do you want to do?"

"We will never beat them one on one. We're too outnumbered."

"So we pick 'em off. One by one."

"That is only good for the few stragglers. It won't work for them all. They will get on to us before long."

"At least we can make the match more even."

"Yes. We can do that. We should also send warning to the community. They can prepare."

"If we can get their numbers down, we'll have a chance."

"Okay, but we've got to control those fires. If the Gotts don't get us the flames will."

"How."

"Take fifteen of your group and have them try to divert or put out the flames after the Gotts pass by. It's not much but it will give us a little time. Maybe the wind will change?"

"And you?"

"I'll go with the rest and try to thin the Gotts down. Then it will be left to a fight in the community. We will attack from above and below. If the community is prepared it will be over before these Gotts realize what is hitting them."

"We'll join in from behind after we deal with the fires."

"Okay."

"Okay. Let's go"

"It is a good sun." Quei clasped his friends shoulder.

"A good sun."

Both then carefully left their meeting place to set their plans into action. From trunk to trunk they went.

It did not take them long to gather together the other Dwellers. Thodox picked his fifteen. They would do what they could and then follow to help. They left quickly. Quei then instructed the remaining Dwellers, and sent them out to do their duties. They went in pairs. One would search, while the other aimed and shot. They were to pick off the Gotts who were the most vulnerable. This meant any Gott who was on his own or away from the main Troop as they traversed through the forest. It should not be too difficult a task. The Gotts were so clumsy and confident that they were spreading out away from each other in the forest.

Once a susceptible Gott was found away from the main Troop, the Dwellers would use their slings to silently hurl the jagged stone that they projected. Though the Dwellers were a tribe of peace, they were marksmen with their slings. They would place a jagged edge stone within the sling and then after gyrating it four times over their head would let it go in the direction of the target. The stone made no noise. There was just the thud of it striking the head of the intended Gott, as it hit its mark, followed by the sinking sound as he fell dead to the forest floor. The stone sling was lethal.

One by one the Dwellers progressed. The Gotts were totally unaware of being stalked. They were still making noise and setting the forest aflame as they marched. Over the period from their first entering the forest, to now, at the mid sun, almost a quarter of their number had vanished. In order to continue their elimination, the Dwellers would now have to get very close to the main section of the Troop. Only a few of the Gotts had fallen to the stone sling. Tree by tree they progressed, waiting for any opportunity to slay more of the Gott Troop. There was just half a sunrise's journey to the community.

In the closer range, the Dwellers filled their slings with several stones and used them as clubs. They would stealthily wait, then jump out from behind their concealment and crack a Gott's head. One hit, and the other dragged the victim back behind a tree trunk to be left out of sight as the rest of the Troops walked on. There was so much smoke now, that it helped to cloak both Dweller and slain Gott. The burning of the forest by these stupid Gotts, had inadvertently assisted the Dwellers.

It was not taking long to thin the Troop. Its presence was becoming less powerful. The Gotts soon sensed this change and began checking their numbers. There started a calling out from Gott to Gott above the burning and traipsing noise that they made through the wood. They would call and after waiting what was enough time to answer, called again. Fear was setting in and could be heard in the tone of the calling out. The slain Troopers were finally being missed. The fear within this Troop was intensified by the legends of the forest. Each Gott knew all the stories of the mysterious creatures that lived within this forest. How they were never seen or heard; that they were cannibalistic and stalked their prey silently. The fact that many of their number had not responded and were not accounted for, added to their anguish.

As the Dwellers eliminated each Gott that they found, there was now a visible down sizing of the Troop. A shrinking that was not noticed by any of them till now. The loss was more substantial, and the Troop was becoming more uneasy. They were calling more often to locate their missing comrades. They did not, however, go back in search of them. They just called out their names while moving on. Their pace quickened as a mild paranoia set in. They did not want to meet these forest creatures by themselves. They would rather stay grouped together. The confidence that had existed in this Troop as it had crossed into the land of the Dwellers, was now vanishing along with its compliment.

Almost half the Gott Troop had been eliminated over the distance from the river to the outskirts of the forest community. The advance warning from Quei and Thodox, had allowed the Dwellers to camouflage and prepare. Any access to the treetop level was concealed or cut off. No matter how many Gotts arrived they would be disadvantaged. They would not be able to discover them or the community.

All the Dwellers left the ground level and were

placed in strategic positions all along the upper community. Some Dwellers were setting large vine nets, which could be dropped upon the enemy below. Others, had baskets of rocks that would be thrown down. There was hot tree sap in huge containers that was to be poured upon the Gotts. Finally, there were the stone slings which the more experienced Dwellers would use to fend off these intruders. It would be a difficult battle for the unsuspecting Gotts. The Dwellers would not allow any to survive. They had to protect the secret of their location and existence.

By the time the Troop had arrived at the location of the community, as shown by the map that Merm had made for them, only thirty remained. They were very unsettled. Smoke from their fires was billowing all around. The wind had changed and now the Gotts were being hampered by their own fire. They had stopped and grouped together. The impact of their reduction was startling. They were not yet aware that they were being watched from above.

Quei and his Dwellers were close behind as the Troop entered their ambush. They had managed to thin the numbers of the Troop, and then followed the remaining Gotts to their forest community. Thodox and his group of fifteen had caught up with Quei just before they all reached the community. Both groups of Dwellers huddled together behind a large trunk and listened. Quei and Thodox spoke:

"We have managed to slow the blaze, but it will require a larger effort."

"Good. There're down to half."

"I like these odds better."

"Yes. They don't realize what is above. When they are well into the community, it will begin. Let's place ourselves around them, hidden to their view. While they are taking cover from above, we will attack from behind. Use the slings first. Hand to hand will be impossible. Do not let any escape."

"No, we won't."

"As soon as you are in place... wait till they start from above. Then attack."

"Okay."

The discussion was brief. All understood what was required of them. One by one they ran to their positions, using the trees to screen their movements. The Gotts were being slowly surrounded as they discussed their predicament and consulted the map to get some bearings. The Dwellers above and below waited with their slings in hand, for the fight to begin.

Suddenly and without any warning the tree top Dwellers began the onslaught. It surprised the Gotts below, who did not understand the source of the assault. They tried to back out of the line of fire, but every way they turned another barrage hit them. In a panic, they began to retreat back along the way they had come into the area. Quei's group was ready, and the Gotts were met with many stone projectiles. The combination from below and above was decimating the Troop. A few Gotts managed to break away, but were rapidly stopped by Thodox's group. The fighting was one sided. The battle lasted only moments, though it seemed an eternity to those involved. The Gotts were successfully ensnared. The air was filled with projectiles, nets, and boiling sap. There were cries of Gotts from the agony of being struck, caught and scalded. It looked like a scene from a horrible nightmare.

After the last Gott had fallen dead to the ground, there was a long silent pause. The reality of the scene now slowly sank into each Dweller. They had beaten back this enemy.

From out of their forest concealment, Quei and Thodox emerged. They proceeded to walk through the battleground and as they went, examined the fallen Gott bodies. Everyone of the

Dwellers carefully watched as they traversed the battlefield. When it was certain that no Gott had survived, Quei and Thodox raised up their arms and made a joyous whooping sound. This was echoed throughout the community. There were cheers from ground and tree top. All Dwellers were proud that, through their preparations, the fight had gone fast and well. Though the initial threat was over, they each privately knew that there may be others to come. For now they could revel in their victory. The next time they may not be so lucky.

The sunrise ended as it had begun. The Dweller's and their secret were still in place. The rumors of the disappearance of this Troop of Gotts would eventually add to the myths of the creatures of Burning Forest. It would be a tremendous deterrent.

Chapter 11.

"Who enters? Speak or you will not safely pass."

The Trooper of the outer gate to Aug had seen these three ride up from the distance. It was the sunset. He could see that these riders were Gotts, but from the distance could not individually identify them. Whoever they were, they had come a long way. Their mounts were foaming at the mouth; their riders worn and even more unkempt than the usual Gott. As they had come to the gate, the Gate Trooper had called out. One of the riders replied:

"I will go where I want, Trooper! Send word of my arrival to the Garrison Commander, have him meet me in the Great Hall." Merm had no patience left. He spoke with the tone of a leader. The Gate Trooper recognized the tone immediately, but not the speaker of the words. He was confused,

"Who are you?"

"This is your Lord, you fool!" blurted out one of the two Troopers who had successfully completed the journey from the Burning Forest to Aug, with Lord Merm.

"My Lord. Is that really you?" came nervously in disbelief.

"Hurry up you slag. Open the gate, and follow my command, lest you want to be posted to the cells."

The cells were the dungeons deep beneath the castle. No one wanted to be posted there. It was full of vermin and the rank of the place stayed with, and ate away at you.

"Right away, my Lord."

The Gate Trooper, though not totally convinced, did not question them further. Immediately he pulled the levers from his position atop the gate, and the huge stone wall that blocked the entrance to Aug swung open. Merm did not wait for the gate to completely open, but slid by as soon as there was enough room to squeeze past. He was followed by the two Troopers. Before he resumed the ride he shouted to the Gate Trooper:

"Send my message."

"Right away, my Lord."

The three then rode off from the outer gate. The Gate Trooper was astonished to have met his Lord this way. He had not been informed of his arrival from Norkleau. It was embarrassing. If indeed it was Lord Merm. Perhaps it was a surprise inspection. He had better notify the Garrison Commander before Merm arrived at the main gate of Aug, just in case.

Merm rode hard along the path to the inner gate of Aug. It was a rocky barren pathway. On all sides was a clear view of Aug. The castle imposingly stood out from the mountainous landscape. There was a long winding pathway which followed the mountainside, leading away to the dark edifice. Here and there was a plateau with tents struck upon it. These were the outskirts of the garrison. The place was filthy with the mess of many encamped along the path. There were Troopers all along the way: sitting, drinking, relaxing, fighting. Refuse lay everywhere. Coupled with the overcast sky, the whole area appeared dark and desolate.

Merm loved the sight. Though exhausted from the ride, he was exhilarated to be back amongst the terrain of the Gott Mountains and Aug. He was at home in this sty. As he rode, the occasional Trooper recognized his rank and saluted. Merm felt powerful again.

By the time Merm and the two Troopers arrived at the inner second gate, the Garrison Commander had been given Merm's message. The Garrison Commander had then immediately sent out orders to all the Gate Troopers to prepare and watch for the arrival of the Lord. He then commanded all his Sub Commanders to meet in the Great Hall to greet their Lord. Everything was so unexpected that there was a great hustle to make certain that nothing was out of place.

Food and drink was ordered to be taken to the Great Hall. The Lord would want refreshment after his long ride from Norkleau. When everything had been organized, the Garrison Commander went to his chamber to put on a clean dress uniform, he wondered as he prepared, why Lord Merm had not come by way of the northwestern path, but did not spend long on this thought. Merm would be here soon and there was still much to do. He checked himself once over and then left his chamber.

The inner gate was opened. As Merm and his party rode through, the particular Gate Trooper saluted. Word of the Lord's arrival had begun to filter through to all the Troopers. Many had lined the pathway from the inner gate to the main castle entrance to welcome their Lord. They carried torches as it was now getting dark. The firelight flickered. They lined the edge of the path through the main market courtyard as if it was a processional. This helped to lead the weary three to the castle. Once they arrived, the Garrison Commander and a small welcoming party were standing waiting to greet them. The three stopped. Merm dismounted and was approached by the Garrison Commander.

"My Lord. Welcome. I have food and drink prepared."

"Good. It has been a long ride." Merm turned to the two Troopers who were still mounted, "Dismissed."

"My Lord."

"My Lord." Both were led off by one of the Garrison Commander's party.

"May I ask the purpose of this unexpected visit, my Lord?" Merm was now walking up the stairs, followed by the Garrison Commander just behind. As they climbed the stairs, the Commander was privately ushering, with his hands out of the Lord's view, the others to leave.

"In the Hall," was all that Merm said. It was done in a gruff manner. The Commander was concerned that he was about to be reprimanded for something, or worse...replaced.

They both climbed the thirty steps to the main doors of the castle. They were opened and two Troopers stood, as doormen, saluting. Merm ignored them. This was his usual custom and was not considered effrontery by anyone. He walked on and into the main castle hallway.

Down the large hallway which was more like a corridor, Merm and the Garrison Commander went, not a word was spoken. All along the corridor was placed a ceremonial guard, and next to each, protruding from stands at shoulder height, were flaming torches. Each Trooper stood rigidly beside the torches tucked away in little wall alcoves. They looked like ancient museum statues on display. They blended in with the walls which were made from a dark stone.

There was a cloistered feel to the hallway. There were no openings to the outside. It had a cathedral-like ceiling, which was very high. The light from the burning torches was the only light that ever radiated against it. There was black soot from the torches stretching up in jagged lines and disappearing into the dark pointed ceiling.

The hallway ran straight for about fifty lengths. There was a sameness to it. The only sound that could be heard was of the footsteps of Merm and his Commander being placed solidly upon the polished rock floor. They reverberated off the floor and walls, giving the impression of many more feet than there were walking upon it.

At the far end of the hallway were two more Troopers. They each stood to one side of a set of opened dark wood doors. This was the entrance to the Great Hall. These doors were half a length thick and ten lengths high. They were massive. Large black ornate hinges held their sturdy mass to the rock wall entrance. Two diamond shaped handles, placed about two lengths up its length, struck the eye. The two Troopers each had one hand upon the handles and were holding the doors, which were swung inward, and open.

Merm and the Commander entered. Inside the Great Hall there was a tremendous open space. All the surfaces were made of rock. The Hall was easily fifty lengths wide and one hundred long. From the floor to the top of the arched ceiling was another seventy five lengths. There were no openings to the outside at the lower levels of the Hall, but at the top of the arched ceiling there was a series of slits running horizontally that opened to the outside. Very little light found its way through these slits, though plenty of air did circulate. There were lit torches every ten lengths along the sides of the Hall and several large candelabrums hanging centrally off a straight long heavy black chain draping from the ceiling, from the Throne to the main entry.

On the left side, at the far end, was a pulpit raised several lengths above the floor level. There was a stairwell in the wall adjacent to it that was obviously the only way up to it. To the right of the pulpit, and central to the Great Hall was a raised platform area with a huge Throne placed upon it. It was the focal point of the Hall. Behind the Throne were two small closed doors. Further to the right of the Throne and these doors, was another stairwell with steps that led down to the sub levels.

There were eleven Gotts standing waiting to the right side of the raised platform as Merm and the Garrison Commander entered and made their way through the Great Hall. When they were nearing the raised platform area, the eleven were motioned by the Garrison Commander to approach the Throne. All that could be heard was the noise of a multitude of boot steps.

Merm stepped up onto the Throne platform and

proceeded to sit upon his symbol of Office. The Garrison Commander stood next to it on his right, and the eleven other Gotts were again beckoned by him, to step forward onto the platform to be presented to the Lord. They each stepped up and bowed their heads. These were the various Commanders of Aug.

As they bowed, the farther right door behind the Throne opened, and two female Gotts meekly passed through. One carried a tray with food and drink, the other a small table. They brought them to the Garrison Commander, who silently motioned them to put the table to the left of the Lord with the tray upon it. They did so without word. Females were not allowed to speak in the presence of their Lord. Once the tray was placed both females bowed and backed out through the way they had entered. The door closed. Merm picked up a large tankard that was on the tray and gulped the drink. He got more on him than in him. Satisfied, he placed the tankard back in its place and directed his attention to the waiting Commanders who were still bowed in respect and waiting. Then looking away, started:

"Commander Citol."

"Yes, my Lord." The Garrison Commander turned to face Merm from the right side.

"Are these all the Commanders?"

"Yes Lord."

"Good."

Citol had been made Garrison Commander after the failure of the invasion of the Southlands. Ruel was demoted as punishment for his poor council to Merm the eve before the invasion, and stood amongst the eleven. It was a difficult insult to bear, but he did. Only Citol had warned of the possible defeat. When the defeat occurred and Merm was trapped, Citol had also been one of the few Commanders that was not quick to take advantage of his absence.

"Ruel."

"Yes Lord." Ruel alone looked up.

"Inform your Troops to watch for outsiders. They are to be stopped and brought before me. *Without fail.*" Merm stressed this last section.

Ruel was insulted by the implication. He bowed his head without expression or comment.

"At ease." Merm had forgotten to acknowledge the reverence of the bow. "All of you." Immediately the eleven raised their heads.

"I want the rest of you to organize a search. All Southworlders in Aug are to be rounded up and brought before me. Every part of Aug must be searched for outsiders. Especially here in the castle. Double your guards. Immediately."

"But Lord, there will be complaint." Citol carefully interjected. The other Commanders waited to observe the results of such a public questioning of the Lord's wishes. There was a pause. Merm was considering Citol's words.

"Tell them it is for their own safety. That there has been a threat against them, and we wish to protect them."

"Yes Lord." Citol had been heard. The Commanders saw that he had Merm's favor.

"Do not let any escape. Search well. Entry to and from the castle must be secured. No one may come or go without my written command."

"Yes, my Lord."

"Yes, my Lord."

"Yes, my Lord."

"Yes, my Lord."

"Yes, my Lord."

"Yes, my Lord."

"Yes, my Lord."

"Yes, my Lord."

"Yes, my Lord."

"Yes, my Lord."

"Yes, my Lord." the Commanders all replied some together, some overlapping, others separately.

"Then, dismissed."

They each bowed and took their leave. Only Citol remained.

"My Lord." Citol initiated.

"Yes."

"What of the secret ways within the castle."

"Secret Ways? Do you know of them?"

"I know that they may exist, but not exactly where. Should we not place Troopers in every area of the castle to keep watch?"

"Yes that is wise. Even I do not know the location of the all the possible hidden passages. Of the ones that I do, we will place Troopers immediately. We will not speak to them of hidden passages. These things are not to be known. You will not mention this to anyone."

"Never, my Lord."

"Then place as many Troopers as you can inside every room of the castle. We will greet any uninvited user of *secret* passages."

"Yes Lord." Citol could see that Merm was impressed with his suggestion.

Citol had learnt of the secrets of the castle of Aug quite accidentally while examining the ancient plans. He had been familiarizing himself with all aspects of his new garrison command after his appointment. He wanted to know of any weaknesses that may be kept out from the normally available information that an ex-Garrison Commander would have presented to him upon being promoted to the position. He did not trust Ruel to be offering the fullest disclosure of data. In fact, he expected any materials from him to be flawed and laced with misinformation that might lead to his own demotion. Citol decided to review and check all that he could. In terms of the castle, he had referred to the ancient plans and checked every room that was shown on them. There were several instances where rooms were narrower or not quite as shown on the plans. He assumed that there must be a reason for these discrepancies. He had gone into the oldest archives to trace the variances. No other Garrison Commander had ever bothered to be so thorough.

The plans were all intact and covered with dust. Citol had managed to discover that there were false walls with passages behind them, that could be used to hide in, if the castle was over-run by an enemy. No other commander had ever bothered to find these secrets, though they were clearly waiting in the archives for any with access to see. It seemed logical, now that Merm was concerned with uninvited intruders, that there may be ways in and out of Aug other than through the gates. He did not know where they were, just that they may exist. Not to protect against such possibilities, was foolish. It was his duty to inform the Lord of such potentialities.

"Make the arrangements. After I eat I will go to my chamber. Wake me if there are any developments."

Merm was treating Citol as he would have Rmont. He suddenly missed him. It was the first time he had been in Aug since losing Rmont. In his mind, he had half expected to find him here waiting for him, but he wasn't. He was gone. Citol was not Rmont, but he reminded Merm of him.

"Yes Lord." Citol bowed and walked to the door that the females had brought the food through, opened it and left. When the door was pulled shut, Merm was left alone in the Great Hall.

"Let me have them now." Merm spoke out to the empty air, and took in the magnitude of the place. The echo of his voice gradually distancing.

He brought his attention to the tray of food and drink to his left. He was suddenly reminded of his hunger. Without using utensils, he tore at the food. It was a revolting sight. He shoved fistful after fistful of food into his large mouth. Pieces of food stuck to his beard, and he did not bother to wipe them away. He just shoveled more food in, and swallowed it after it was barely chewed.

In this solitude the real animal within him was revealed. He ate till there was nothing left on the tray, then picked up the tankard to wash it all down. He drained the liquid and threw the tankard to the ground. He stood up and belched. He rustled his left hand through his facial hair to remove any particles of food. He shook like a Dolog, then proceeded to the door behind the Throne, to the left of the service entry. He opened it, and stepped into the long hallway that led to his private chamber which was not far from there.

The hallway was big enough for only one to travel through. It was dark, except for a torch that was lit and placed on the wall at its end about twenty lengths away. Merm made his way and stopped at the torch. He opened the door whose spot the torch marked, and entered into a large chamber.

The room was large and well lit by torches. It was constructed from solid rock and there was no decoration upon it. It was Spartan, containing a bed, chair and large stone table. There were two openings to the outside in the southwestern wall, that in the sunset, piercing red beams of the setting sun shone through. These windows ran from

floor to ceiling. Great streaks of red fell throughout the chamber. Merm walked up to them and
gazed out to the horizon.

His chamber was on the cliff side of the castle.
From the windows could be seen part of the
northeastern section of Aug and the lands to the
north and south west. There was a drop of over a
thousand lengths to the ground directly below his
chamber location in this mountain top fortress,
and then a huge valley leading off to the lesser
foothills and Lake of Choices in the distance of
the southwest. He could see a tremendous panora-
ma. He was pleased to be home and safe in Aug.
He wondered where the thieves were; if they were
near by. He felt prepared for their arrival. He took
the Key off the chain from around his neck, and
his small dagger from his boot, as he crossed to
the table. He held the knife steadily upon the table
with his left hand, and placed the Key on it with
his right. The Key began to spin around and
around. It would not steady.

"They must be here." Merm said out loud. He
took the Key and placed it back around his neck
hidden under his tunic. He went back to the windows and gazed out into Aug.

"Where are you?"

After several moments, he took his eyesight

from the vista and walked to his bed. It was large and fluffy. It was inviting. Merm got unto the bed and closed his eyes. He needed sleep. He could worry no more. He was terribly worn by the sunrise's journey. He thought briefly of his ally before losing consciousness.

- - - - - - - - - - - - - -

"Oh no!" Eruinn blurted out. He was peering through the peep hole and into the Great Hall of Aug while the others discussed their next moves.

"What is it?" Thiunn responded first. The others stopped talking and waited for Eruinn's answer.

"Gotts. One, two...eight...eleven...thirteen. Thirteen Gotts." He pushed his left eye hard against the hole. "One looks like...It's Merm. He's seated on the Throne and talking to the others."

"What?!" Darla scrambled to Eruinn's side. "What else do you see."

"No...nothing."

"Here, let me see." she pushed him aside and placed her eye at the hole. "How did he know?"

"Know what?" Julian asked.

"How did he know to come here to Aug? To find us?"

There was silence. Then Buold offered a reason.

"He must have help."

266

"The *Evil*?" Darla returned her sight to them.

"Yes, or a powerful talisman."

"Like the Key. He has the Key. The Key must have been drawn here by the *Passwords*." Julian knew this from within his ancient awakening. "The Key has found the books and us."

"But how would Merm know this?" Thiunn had not made the connection.

"The *Evil* has helped. Just as it has been helping him find us all along. Ever since my entry into the lower forest I have felt a strong dark presence. It has been watching and following our movements."

"Then why hasn't Merm found us in here?" Eruinn wondered out loud.

"I don't know, why he hasn't. There must be limits to his knowledge and the help from the *Evil*." Julian considered this, as Buold added.

"There is a way to find out."

"How." Julian did not understand.

"When I was told to help guide you to this place, I did not understand why. You all know the way to Aug. I could have just told you to come here, and search the Great Hall for the Marks. Now I understand. Through my dream travel I can discover things without being seen or heard. I can find out what we need to hear. I can go in there and find out what they know."

"Really?" Thiunn was intrigued.

"Yes. I will need to concentrate. No matter what happens, do not disturb me, any of you."

"Is there anything else we can do?" Darla inquired.

"Yes. Remain here till I return. Do not leave."

They all nodded in the light of the illuminator. Buold then sat cross legged and placed the palms of his hands one upon each bent knee cap. Closing his eyes he hummed a steady tone. They watched as he slowly drifted into his dream state. Then he jerked, which startled them. They wondered if he was alright, but they did not disturb him.

Buold jerked into the dream state. He saw the Southlanders as he rose up and out of his own body. Gradually he moved up and then through the solid rock into the Great Hall. He directed his travel to the Throne where the Gotts were talking and positioned himself to listen:

"Commander Citol."

"Yes, my Lord." the Gott to the right of Merm *spoke.*

"Are these all the Commanders?"

"Yes Lord."

"Good."

"Ruel."

"Yes Lord." One of the Gotts with the bowed head looked up.

"Inform your Troops to watch for any outsiders. They are to be stopped and brought before me. Without fail."

"At ease. All of you."

"I want the rest of you to organize a search. All Southworlders in Aug are to be rounded up and brought before me. Every part of Aug must be searched for outsiders. Especially here in the castle. Double your guards."

"But Lord, there will be complaint." the Gott to Merm's right spoke again.

"Tell them it is for their own safety. That there has been a threat against them, and we wish to protect them."

"Yes Lord."

"Do not let any escape. Search well. Entry to and from the castle must be secured. No one may come or go without my written command."

"Yes, my Lord." the Gotts all replied some together, some overlapping, others separate.

"Then dismissed."

They each bowed and took their leave. Only the one Gott to his right remained.

"My Lord." was initiated.

"Yes."

"What of the secret ways within the castle."

"Do you know of them?"

"I know that they may exist, but not exactly where. Should we not place Troopers in every area of the castle to keep watch?"

"Yes that is wise. Even I do not know the location of the all the possible hidden passages. Of the ones that I do, we will place Troopers immediately. We will not speak to them of hidden passages. These things are not to be known. You will not mention this to anyone."

"Never, my Lord."

"Then place as many Troopers inside every room of the castle. We will greet any uninvited user of secret passages."

"Yes Lord."

"Make the arrangements. After I eat I will go to my chamber. Wake me if there are any developments."

"Yes Lord." The Gott bowed and left.

Buold watched and listened as the foul Gott ate. He was repulsed by his barbarianism. Soon Merm had finished and rose. He went to a door behind the Throne and exited, Buold followed. After several lengths Merm went through another door and entered a bed chamber. Buold assumed this was

Merm's private chamber. Merm crossed the room and stood silently staring out of a large window for a long period. Suddenly, he pulled a chain from around his neck and took off a Key. Next he bent over and removed a small dagger from his boot, and crossed to a table. Merm held the knife steady upon the table with his left hand and placed the Key on it with his right. The Key began to spin around and around. It would not steady.

"They must be here." Merm said out loud. *"Where are you?"*

"So that is how he knew." Buold thought to himself. He had seen enough, it was time to return to the others.

- - - - - - - - - - - - -

Dorluc was waiting for Merm to sleep. He wanted to influence him more. He had viewed the journey from beyond the river through the forest and on to Aug, but he had not discovered anything of the thieves. He was helpless to do anything more. Everything now depended upon Merm locating the *Password*s before the Chosen Ones could dispose of them. Dorluc had no idea where that might be, though he knew that the Key had pointed in the direction of Aug. When Merm had used the Key in the castle and it spun around, it meant that they were there, under his very nose. Merm must be told. As Merm drifted into sleep Dorluc entered his dreaming mind.

"*They are here.*"

"The thieves?"

"*Yes. When the Key continues to spin that means they are here. Find them.*"

"I have placed my Troops. They will not be able to enter without my knowledge.

"*Do not be so sure. They have the Magic of the books. They will use it to hide them.*"

"Every part of the castle is watched. They will not be able to enter."

"*When you find them, take the books. Insert the Key between them and say these words: 'Fro me her te bij ku.' These will unleash the Magic of the books. You will then be invincible.*"

"I will."

"*Do not sleep long. They will soon try to complete their purpose.*"

Merm was exhausted, and so moaned an affirmative response. There was nothing else Dorluc could do. Merm needed some rest or he would be of no use. He left Merm's mind and returned to the Land. There using the view screen, he would continue to search for any sign of the Chosen Ones. They were here somewhere. He felt their proximity.

- - - - - - - - - - - - - -

Buold's body jerked again. It had been still for a long time. Darla was becoming concerned for his safety. She wondered if this movement was an indication of Buold encountering trouble within his dream travel. This motion worried them all. It intensified. Suddenly Buold's head began to sway in large slow circles. It was a rhythmic process. Then, in a quick total body spasm, his eyes popped wide open. There was life in his sight. He was returned.

"They know. Merm has a Key which shows our location. He has made plans and organized his Troops to watch and guard against our entry. You must act now, or it will be impossible to complete your task."

They all remained silently seated in the passageway as each absorbed the meaning of this announcement. There were frowns of frustration upon their faces. This was an unexpected discovery. How could it have happened so easily? They could not seem to get away from Merm or the *Evil*.

No one spoke. Julian, like all of them, sat. He did not know how to react. Buold was still recovering from his travel. He rose up and into the light of the illuminator, stretched his limbs to limber them up from the tension of the dream state. He wanted to help hurry them back to waking life. They were slightly numb and tingly. This always happened after a dream travel. It took time to re attach the consciousness back to the myriads of nerves and senses of the body that they had temporarily been detached from. In his early experiences he had often gone into panic at this uncomfortableness, but quickly learnt to control this instinct and grew to patiently understand it and wait for the eventual recovery to complete itself.

As Buold stretched, the others sat dismayed, not certain what they should do next. After several moments of total silence amongst them, a voice spoke out in Julian's head:

"Find the Marks upon the Throne."

Suddenly Julian remembered what he had been told by his 'father', after his fall into the river; that the Key would be found by the *Evil,* and not by him; that he was not to worry about Merm getting it out of the river; that he should instead travel to Aug with the *Passwords*; that 'all' would be joined in Aug. This was the way it was meant to be. Julian took a breath and let out a sigh. His mood was changed. He broke the silence:

"Maybe this is not bad."

"Not bad?" Darla spoke as Thiunn and Eruinn regarded their Uncle in an amazed manner.

"No. This is the way it is meant to be."

"Meant to be?" Darla continued.

"We must go into the Great Hall, and find the Marks of Stone. They are upon the Throne." Julian held a gazed stare as he spoke. He was connecting to his inner knowledge. He sounded as if he was reading the information as he spoke. All except Buold understood.

"What about the Troopers and Merm?" Eruinn asked.

"It will be up to you to stop them."

"How long?"

"I'm not sure, just keep them away till I find the Marks."

"Then what?" Thiunn asked.

"I...I don't quite know, but there is something..." Julian's words trailed off. Darla broke in. She understood that this was a part of the ancient knowledge within Julian. She suddenly felt close to him.

"Then we should go now, and try to get to the Throne before the Troopers are placed. There may only be a few moments. Let's not waste them here. Thiunn. Eruinn. Help me with the door."

They all moved quickly. It was the only opportunity that they would have to complete their task.

Buold joined in and helped as they pushed the symbols of the musical unlocking mechanism. Everything was becoming more clear to them now. They were so close to the end. They could sense it. As they pushed the symbols, there sounded a short melody and the door opened from the passageway onto the pulpit. It was a slow process. They carefully waited. They all kept out of view from the pulpit area. There might be Troopers that they had not seen through the peep hole already placed in the Great Hall. The noise would alert them.

When the door had opened to its fullest, Darla was first to check the safety of their exiting. She leaned out and surveyed the area by sight and sound. It seemed safe, so one by one they exited to the pulpit and exposure within the Great Hall. Darla was in the lead followed by Eruinn, Thiunn, Buold and Julian. They crept out and huddled together on the pulpit. It was a tight fit for them to remain concealed upon. Julian motioned to Darla who was best positioned.

"Take a look." he used his softest voice. He did not want to take any chances that there might still be a Trooper lurking somewhere within the Great Hall.

Darla, following his suggestion, carefully rose and peeped over the top of the pulpit, into the massive space of the Great Hall.

"It's clear so far." she spoke back in a whisper and remained on guard.

"Good." Julian acknowledged Darla, and then turned to the others to organize their descent to the main level of the Great Hall,

"We'll go down the stairs one by one. Then once we hit the main level, Eruinn you keep an eye on the main doors, Thiunn the stairs to the cells below, Buold the doors behind the Throne. I'll go with Darla. Ready?" as he had directed he used motions to point the various locations that they were to proceed to and watch from. They all nodded their understanding and acceptance.

With Darla and Julian watching, they began their descent of the pulpit stairs. Eruinn, Thiunn and Buold moved down ahead, and were soon followed by Darla and Julian. One by one they went, till they had come to the entry of the Great Hall. The stairwell opened widely onto it. They paused for a moment to check for Troopers, then they all crossed the distance to where the raised Throne platform began. They stopped and instinctively crouched. They each scanned the entrances to the Great Hall. There was nothing to conceal them from discovery. They were not comfortable with being so exposed. They all felt extremely vulnerable. Their hearts were pounding and perspiration was beginning to pour from them. They waited. Each wiped the areas where sweat was beading upon their faces. Julian and Darla crossed to the Throne. The others crossed to their positions.

"What are we looking for?" Darla asked after they had arrived at the Throne.

"Marks of Stone…" Julian was examining the large edifice with his eyes as he answered. Before he added to his answer Darla said:

"Craft mark of the Stoneman. A chisel, a hammer, a shield of old and the Key."

Julian briefly paused and looked at her impressively:

"You know the Marks?"

"Yes." she moved closer to the Throne to help in the search.

The Throne was cut from one piece of very large tan-ish colored stone. The type of rock found in the Southlands. It was very large. Much larger than any other inhabitant of any of the Worlds. Only a Gott could fit onto it comfortably. It had a solid base of smooth stone. There were ornate carvings of pictograms on its surface. These pictograms were not like the ones of the passageways of Norkleau. They were foreign in meaning. Upon this base carved out of one solid piece of stone, was the seat. There were solid arms and a solid high back. All were of the same quarried stone, ornately carved and of one piece.

Unknown to them, the Throne had been brought here by the earliest ancestors of the Gotts at the time when they had started to build the castle. Gott legend said that it had been taken from a great temple. Perhaps the temple of Tika, it was never confirmed, but had become part of the lore just the same, and a symbol of the might and right of the Gott to conquer all other worlds. It had been here in the Great Hall in the castle of Aug for a long time. Over time the castle had been added to and changed, but the Throne had always stood in this exact spot. Superstitions arose that upon the moving of the Throne, the Gott Empire would crumble. So it was never moved. Eventually, as an assurance against such a possibility that would work to undermine the Gott morale, the Throne had been carefully and secretly secured to the stone floor. No accident could cause it to move and thereby fulfill the legend. Though the Gotts were no longer the Empire that they once were, the illusion was maintained, at least in terms of the symbolism of the Throne. As long as the Throne was in place there was still a chance to return to greatness. There would be no end to their Empire, only minor lulls. The fact that the Throne was in place provided proof of the value of these beliefs.

"Over here." Julian drew Darla's attention to under the protruding stone seat. He had run his fingers under and along its front edge and in the center of it felt some carvings. Anyone else would have missed their significance considering them just the product of wear or poor workmanship.

"Let me feel." Darla was next to him. Both were now kneeling in front of the Throne. She moved her hand to the place on the underside edge. Julian touched her hand and led it. Her eyes lit up at his touch, but before anything was said, she felt the carvings, and the moment passed unacknowledged.

"What do you think?"

"Could be it?"

Julian got down farther and lowered his body to allow his head to go beneath the level of the seat. He turned his head and gazed under and up.

"A chisel, a hammer, a shield and the Key. The Marks of Stone." just as he said this, and while he was still touching the Marks, Eruinn called out:

"Someone's coming!" The sound of boot steps

approaching from beyond the Great Hall was faintly audible.

"Hide. Help us." Julian's thought called out as his fingers were touching the Marks. He was not calling to anyone in particular. He was just concerned and worried. He hoped that something would prevent their discovery by whoever was coming. His call was to the Magic, not to Darla, Eruinn, Thiunn, or Buold.

"Hide." Darla's voice was the one that called out the words of Julian's thoughts to them all.

Julian drew away his fingers from the touching of the Marks. Hurriedly, Darla and he stepped and crouched together behind the Throne. They motioned for Buold to join them. Buold quickly crossed to them and they all huddled tightly concealed behind the large seat back of the Throne. Julian felt a tingling sensation running throughout his whole body. He thought it must be fear.

Thiunn and Eruinn responded to the danger by placing themselves close to the walls in their respective positions. They tried to hide themselves within the small alcoves that held the torches. It was impossible to blend in with the dark rock walls. They were still in plain view for anyone standing head on within the Great Hall, but from the side, they would not be seen. They would be hidden in their alcoves by the shadows of the dark walls. Their hope was that the light which was dim in the Great Hall, would help to enshroud them. Each, in their place of hiding, prepared as the boot steps came closer.

The sound of the boot steps soon stopped outside. All their eyes focused upon the diamond shaped handles of the main doors. They saw the handle on the right move, and heard the creaking of the large wood door as it opened enough to allow the head of a Trooper to look into the Great Hall. They all held their breath remaining motionless and tensed. The Trooper reconnoitered the Great Hall, and then listened for a few moments. The tension was high amongst them. Then the Trooper shrugged, and drew his head back, as he slowly pulled the large door shut. He had not sighted any of them. There were one or two more steps, then silence. The Trooper was obviously standing guard at the front of the doors, outside from them! What good fortune.

Eruinn winked at Thiunn, who in turn waved to Darla that the coast was clear. They all sighed relief. There was still a chance that they could complete their task unfettered. They waited a little longer just to be certain that there would be no other Troopers arriving. When it was clear that there were none, they all came out from their concealment and gathered around the Throne. They spoke in quiet tones.

- - - - - - - - - - - - - -

Just as the episode in Julian's cottage in Jard, when Darla had touched the craft mark of the Stoneman on the fireplace mantle and called for help, Julian's call was now heard. This sudden drain in the Magic of the Balance drew other eyes their way. Julian's calling had reached the Magic. It began to envelop all of the Chosen and set a tone in the air of the Great Hall that would assure any investigator that all was well, that there was nothing out of the ordinary in its midst, and that they should go back. Go out. This response was not noticeable to any of the five, though it was affecting them in this situation.

Dorluc had been searching for the thieves since he finished his influencing of Merm. He was troubled that he had not been able to trace any of them. At the point of Julian's calling, the view screen unpredictably jumped to display the scene of the Great Hall and the Throne, but there was no sign of the thieves. No matter how he tried, Dorluc could not budge the view screen from this scene. He became irritated.

"What is wrong?" Dorluc spoke out loud to

himself in anger. He tried to adjust the screen, but it was still of no use.

It then struck him that the view screen would not have focused so firmly on this scene unless there was a tremendous drain of Magic emanating from that place. That could only mean one thing. The Chosen Ones must be there. It was a sensing. They were there. They were the cause of the jumping of the view screen. It was just that they were not visible to the screen. Something was helping them to be kept from his sight. The Magic was cloaking them. Realizing the discovery, Dorluc congratulated himself:

"They are here. This is where they are. I must alert the Gott before it is too late. Wakan! I have found the *Passwords!*"

As Dorluc had all these revelations, he also realized the need to stop or slow the thieves from completing their task. He called to Wakan again:

"Help. Wakan you must use your Magic to reveal the thieves. They are here, but I cannot see them."

There was the forming of the opaque cloud and Wakan appeared before Dorluc.

"Where are they?"

"They are there. In the Great Hall, but they are hidden from the screen. You must slow them while I awake the Gott. There is not much time. Hurry."

"I will stop them!" with that Wakan's cloud and image disappeared from Dorluc and the Land.

Dorluc quickly turned his concentration inward and toward the sleeping consciousness of Merm. Merm was in deep sleep. It did not take long for Dorluc to enter his mind.

"Wake up! They are here! Wake up!" Dorluc *was shouting in Merm's thoughts. "Go to the Great Hall. Stop them! They have the books! Hurry!"*

Merm was tired, but his mind heard and understood Dorluc's cry. It woke up his consciousness. Dorluc repeated:

"Wake up! They are here! Wake up! Go to the Great Hall. Stop them! They have the books! Hurry!"

"Yes!" was all that Merm's mind said.

In moments Merm was awake and cognizant of the emergency. Dorluc remained linked to him. He was pushing Merm to act. Merm forcibly rose from his bed, still a little groggy and yelled for his guards:

"Guards! Guards! Set the alarm! They are in the Great Hall." There was no response.

Merm went to his chamber door and opened it.

There was no Trooper in sight. There was no time to waste, he would not wait. Dorluc would not let him. Merm proceeded to leave the room and go down the narrow hallway to the Great Hall and the thieves. As he awakened more, he felt exhilarated by the chance to find them and the books so soon after his arrival back in Aug. He sensed a duality within him, but in the excitement paid it no attention. At long last everything was coming to fruition. This would be an eve he would long remember.

— — — — — — — — — — — — — —

"That was close." Thiunn started.

"Yes." Julian was relieved.

"Too close. We'd better hurry. What are we to do?" Buold asked.

"Everyone stay close. There must be something about the throne that will help us." Julian was turning his mind inward, searching for the reason that they had all come to the Great Hall.

He was looking for the reason, the purpose. There was something here. Something about the Throne and the Marks of Stone. He wanted to touch them again to feel them. He was being drawn to them. He sensed that there was something special about this Throne and the Marks, but he just couldn't place what it was.

"Keep an eye out, while I examine it more closely." Julian turned to check the Throne and the Marks. He remembered the voice of the river telling him to go to the Marks; that there would be a way; that he must look inward.

"Okay, Uncle Julian. Thiunn and I will..." as Eruinn began to speak, a vast opaque cloud began to form several lengths away toward the main entrance, hovering in mid air.

"Thiunn, Eruinn! The cloud from the cottage! The *Evil*!" Darla was alerting them. She stepped forward off the Throne platform and drew Jewel. Immediately the sword's jewels lit up. She readied herself.

Eruinn and Thiunn recoiled and joined her at her side to face the threat.

"Julian, Get on with it. We'll hold *that* off." Darla whispered as strongly as she could, not wishing to have any unnecessary sound alert the outside Trooper. Julian returned to his scrutiny of the Throne.

Within moments of Darla's words, Wakan's image appeared within the cloud. It was stronger and larger than in the cottage in Jard. It was moving toward them. Eruinn and Thiunn crouched lower in anticipation of its attack. Darla raised Jewel and spoke the ancient words:

"Ici Ni Ban yi. Wrik loo no my trd pir!"

Several beams burst from Jewel. Darla had the sword aimed at the image, and three beams of light shot from Jewel into the cloud. There was an *Evil* laugh as the beams passed through the cloud and hit the diamond shaped handles of entry doors. The noise was rippling as they melted and seized. Moments later there was a cry of pain from the guarding Trooper outside, who had obviously tried to open the door by grabbing the outer handles which were not deformed, but were red-hot from the beams striking on the inside, and severely disfigured his hand. His screams were loud. Other boot steps could now be heard approaching from a distance in response to this commotion, but the door was seized in place. There would be a delay before any could force their entry into the hall. Wakan shot back another beam at the three. Darla raised Jewel to intercept, and a struggle ensued between her Magic and Wakan's.

As soon as Darla and Wakan had engaged, the protective invisibility of the thieves ended. Dorluc would now be able to see them all in the Great Hall, but he was no longer in the Land.

Julian was fumbling around at the Throne. Buold was next to him.

"Be calm. The way is here." he tried to soothe Julian.

"But where? What? If we don't find a way, then 'they' will get the *Passwords*." as Julian finished, the left door in the wall behind the Throne opened.

It was Merm. There was a hesitation as Julian's eyes met Merm's menacing stare. It was unnerving. It was the *Evil*. Merm's eyes were brilliant fiery red. They were no longer the eyes of a mere Gott.

"I have you!" Merm's mouth moved but the voice was slithery and slow. It was as if it was the voice of another using Merm and coming through him.

There was no time for Julian to react. Buold ran toward Merm and grabbed onto his legs, causing the great Gott to fall. The two became entangled.

"Do not play with the female. The one at the Throne must be stopped. Hurry." Merm's voice called out to the cloud, but these words were not heard by anyone in the Great Hall.

"Find the way!" Buold shouted as he wrestled with Merm on the floor.

Julian knelt before the Throne. Without further thought he reached for the Marks with both hands and pushed upward. He strained. Suddenly there was a cracking sound. The seat began slowly sliding up and away from its base and stopped. Julian instantly knew what had to be done.

"Eruinn, Thiunn. Help." Julian called to his nephews to help. It was too heavy for him alone to lift.

Eruinn and Thiunn turned when they were called and understood what was required of them. Darla was engaged, but managed to yell:

"Go!"

Both brother's stood up and rushed to help their Uncle. In moments the three of them were pushing. Julian was in-between. They strained. The seat moved more and more. Suddenly, as they pushed Julian let go one hand and grabbed the *Passwords of Promise* from his shirt. Merm, who was still being hampered by Buold saw this action, and increased his struggle against his shackle. Buold was hit several times, and though hurt, did not let go. Merm was trammeled in place. The more he fought the harder Buold held.

As the seat moved there became enough space to push the Passwords into the opening beneath the seat. Without questioning his decision, Julian squeezed the *Passwords* in, as he let go and they fell into the space, he spoke the ancient words:

"Ic noon vra ba, houn gre juk!"

When he had uttered the words, a great yellow-green light began to shine from the opening of the seat from within the base. Merm's voice cried out:

"Noooooooo."

With a final burst of force Merm broke from Buold and scrambling to his feet, ran to the Throne. Dorluc was also crying out.

Not caring about the thieves, Merm applied his strength to the Throne. He wanted to push it open and retrieve the books. Julian, Eruinn and Thiunn fell aside, exhausted. Merm pushed with supernatural strength.

Dorluc, cried out to him from within:

"No. Stop!"

Merm was like one possessed and acting irrational. He ignored the voice. He continued to push. The opening enlarged, and the seat fell hinged back and wide open. A tremendous beam shot upward and filled the room. There was a momentary calm. Everyone other than Merm drew back and shielded their eyes. He stood possessed in front of the opening. The light pouring onto him. He was staring into the opening. He saw the books. He reached down into the light.

The sudden brightness had distracted Wakan and he stopped his own beams. At this instant Darla was freed from their struggle. She fell to the floor blinded by the light from the Throne. Jewel dropped from her grip and flew with a whizzing sound swiftly away from Darla towards the Throne. There was a thud, as Jewel was solidly imbedded into the upper left back of Merm. There was an oozing sound as it pierced through him. Merm reacted by rigidly jerking perfectly upright. He stood motionless and tense. He brought his sight to the bloody blade extruding through the front of his upper chest. The blade had also cut through the chain that held the Key around his neck. Merm raised his hands to try to catch the chain as it fell with the Key away from him and into the lighted opening. He was unable to act fast enough. The Key fell. Merm staggered back two steps suddenly understanding that life was over and he had no control over the situation. Without uttering a word his mouth opened wide. He instantly knew of his duality and betrayal by Dorluc. His stare searched the Great Hall for an answer, but he knew there was none. He toppled over to the hard stone floor, dead. His eyes remained open and popping out of his head in shock.

Just as Wakan was realizing that he should leave this place, there played a seven note melody, and a voice spoke:

"You were warned, but would not heed. We have watched, and hoped you would heed, but you have transgressed again and again. Here is your final punishment." the voice was ancient and aimed at the cloud.

There was a realization of what was about to occur within everyone in the Great Hall. Wakan was caught, he had no opportunity to leave. It was all happening so unpredictably fast. The beam from the seat intensified and the melody became louder and louder as it repeated. The beam surged toward Wakan's cloud and engulfed it.

For several moments all the light from the Throne intensified. The Chosen Ones covered their eyes. They heard a loud cry from Wakan. Then just as the sound and light were almost unbearable, there came a brilliant flash, and all sounds of Wakan were gone.

Cautiously, the Chosen removed their arms from their eyes, and viewed the Great Hall and the Throne. The seat was still open and the yellow-green subdued light radiating from it, filled the Great Hall. They slowly rose. Julian rushed to Buold and helped him up. He was battered, but there was no serious injury. Eruinn and Thiunn were helping Darla. Merm was motionless on the floor to the right of the Throne, face down.

"Chosen Ones." a voice came from above the Throne opening from a faint image that was hovering above. It was of a person not like any of their Worlds. It was a kindly image.

"You have honored your word. Come. It is time to go."

"Go where?" Julian asked.

"Back to where it started. Back to a new beginning. Enter the light. Come, it is safe."

A banging and shouting upon the main doors of the Great Hall momentarily interrupted the conversation. Troopers were trying to force their way in. In moments they would all be captured. Julian did not want to go back through the passageway. There was no other alternative than to listen and trust the image before them.

"Trust in your self. Come." the image invited them with its words and gestures.

Darla was the first to move. She walked over to Merm and removed Jewel. She kicked his filthy body, spat on him, and then turned her eyes to the Throne opening. She understood what she must do. She trusted the voice. Without a word she stepped up into the Throne opening and slowly went down into the light. Before she went out of view she turned to the others:

"Come on." she encouraged.

Timidly Eruinn, and Thiunn followed after her and stepping into the Throne opening, disappeared into the yellow-green light. It was like a door, a portal into another place.

"Come." the image called to Julian.

Julian turned to Buold.

"Are you coming?"

"No. I cannot enter."

"What do you mean?"

"In my dream, I was told that I could not enter. I will go back through the passageway. It is the only way for me, and this…" he indicated the Throne, "…is yours."

The banging at the main entrance grew louder. The Troopers were making progress. They would soon be inside.

"I hope we meet again soon." Julian did not have time to argue.

"We will. It is good to be with friends."

"With Friends."

Buold crossed to the stairs and went up to the pulpit and the passageway entrance. Julian watched as Buold entered and the door closed after him. Julian then turned his head toward the image that was patiently waiting over the Throne.

He decided. He stepped up and into the Throne opening and disappeared from view.

After all had gone and the Hall was empty, slowly the upper part of the Throne slid back into place and the light that emanated from the seat slowly diminished, till the seat was firmly snapped back into place. All trace of that light and the Chosen Ones in the Great Hall was gone. The space was again lit solely by the torches. It was gloomy.

As the Troopers forced open the doors and flew into the Great Hall ready to battle a terrible enemy, all they found was their Lord dead upon the Throne platform next to a small table in a pool of blood. They would never be able to understand what had transpired there.

Chapter 12.

Mrs. Reed was sitting by the bedside. It was very late and she was tired. She had been there most of the eve and was keeping Lenore company. She was knitting to help pass the time and soothe herself over the tragedy of Lenore. The room was peaceful. A small light on the table next to her, provided a warmth to the scene. Lenore had not yet awakened, and Mrs. Reed was wondering if she ever would. As she knit, she thought of the Lenore that she had come to know in Pers. A lovely vital female. It was so sad to see her end this way. Mrs. Reed sighed and shook her head in pity.

"My poor dear. Why has this happened to you?" she spoke out loud as she concentrated on her knitting, "Of all the Jardians to pick on, why you and your family?"

- - - - - - - - - - - - - -

It was odd. Darla stepped into the opening and down into what she believed were a set of stairs. She was surrounded by the yellow-green light. There was a sound of thunder rolling and crashing somewhere in the distance. The sound of heavy rain was all around her. There was a cool damp breeze, but there was no water or immediate sign of the storm. She was perfectly dry and unaffected by the storm, though the sounds of it were upon her.

Darla continued forward. She had no awareness of the others being behind her. She knew within her that they were near. The image that had invited them in had vanished as soon as she had entered. Again she was not worried by this disappearance. She was more interested in this place. She could not see very far in front, above, or behind her. There was a mist that came to her knees. She walked without knowing what was below it. She could not see her feet in this sea of fog. The yellow-green hue was everywhere. She continued.

After she had taken about thirty steps, she noted a darkness about twenty lengths ahead. It was in the shape of an arched door. She was fascinated and not afraid. The closer she came to it the larger it became. She came within a length of it and could only see blackness. She paused.

"Do not be afraid. It will not harm you." it was the voice of the image.

"You have honored your calling. You are forever Chosen. A new world waits for you."

"Waits?"

"You will take our place and lead them."

"Where?"

"The journey within."

"Just me?"

"No all of you together. You are the Chosen Ones. Enter your future."

Darla took several steps forward. She felt as if she had stepped from one universe to another. She approached the dark arched area and passed into it. Though it was dark, she had no fear. The yellow-green light was now gone. All the sounds of that place behind her were rapidly diminishing, till they were heard no longer. She took a few steps, and then grabbed for Jewel to light her way.

Eruinn and Thiunn went through much the same

experiences as Darla did, except they wondered where this 'shaft' was taking them. Before they knew it, they were stepping through the same dark arched passageway as Darla, unbeknownst to them, had moments before. They strained to see where they were going, using their out-stretched arms to guide them through the dark-ened passage. After several lengths there appeared a strange glowing light straight ahead. A light that was similar to the one of Jewel's gems. They hurried towards the light and without realiz-ing, they stepped out of the passageway and into...

"What kept you?" Darla was sitting on the green leather sofa of their Uncle's cottage. They gave questioning looks to each other and then realized that they had somehow been transported home to Jard in a few moments. They were standing in the fire room. Darla was directly in front of them. They turned to look behind—it was the huge stone fireplace. The passageway they had just been walking in, was nowhere to be found.

"We're home?" Eruinn started.

"In Jard?" Thiunn finished.

"Yes, we are back."

"And Uncle Julian?" Eruinn did not want a repeat of the last time they had been separated in

Norkleau passages.

"He'll be here soon. He was behind you. Thiunn, help me start a fire and get the lights. Eruinn, put on the kettle. We need some tea. We are home. Our journey is over." Darla was elated and pleased that they were all safe and back where they had started. She now understood completely.

- - - - - - - - - - - - - -

Mrs. Reed was still knitting by the bedside, when suddenly she felt a hand grasp her own. She was startled and jumped back, dropping her yarn.

"They're back! My family is back!" Lenore was awake and sitting bolt upright. Mrs. Reed was overjoyed by Lenore's awakening, but tried to calm what she felt was an obviously delirious Lenore.

"Now, there there. Calm yourself. I'm sure your family is back."

"I must go to them." Lenore pulled back her covers and got out of her bed. Mrs. Reed was helpless to stop the determined Lenore, who quickly ran from the room, through the hallway and out the front door of her house. Mrs. Reed, flabbergasted, chased after her.

- - - - - - - - - - - - - -

"Julian. I am proud of you. You have

saved the Balance, and the Evil has been stopped. You are truly a Stoneman and Keeper of Three."

Julian was walking through the yellow-green mist as the voice came to him. He was almost at the dark doorway.

"Father. You knew of all this."

"Yes. It is our calling, and you have honored our name."

"What now?"

"You will go on. You will help to make sure the Evil never returns. The Key and Passwords of Promise are safe and the Balance intact, but there will be others one day. You must prepare our Worlds for them."

"Will you be here to help?"

"I am always here with you. You have but to call. I am amongst the many that you carry. Now go on. Go to your new beginning. Join the others. They will need your strength and knowledge within."

"Thank you father."

"Good bye my son. Remember it is good to be with friends."

"With friends on such a sunrise."

Just as he had finished speaking, Julian stepped through the darkened arched doorway and into his cottage in Jard. Darla, Eruinn, and Thiunn were waiting. They were watching the fireplace as Julian stepped through the 'door' at the location where the craft marks of his father were upon the mantle. It looked as if he had walked out of the small fire that was now burning.

"Uncle Julian!" the nephews exclaimed as they ran to him and hugged him.

Darla was now standing. She was different. Softer and more beautiful. Her eyes were penetrating and fixed upon Julian.

"We are back home, my love."

"We are home." Julian smiled and returned her gaze. The nephews understood. They were all changed. They were the same as they were before but more. They would never be the Jardians who had first started on this adventure just a short while ago, nor did they want to be. They would never be the same again.

She crossed over to him and they all embraced. As they stood there absorbing the emotion, they heard a voice calling out to them from inside the cottage:

"Thiunn... Eruinn... Julian... Darla!" Lenore had seen the smoke from the chimney and doubled her speed as she approached the cottage. It was early morn as she ran into the cottage, she called their names.

"Mother!" the Young Ones replied.

Lenore heard them, and followed the sound. She entered the room, and tears filled her eyes. Her family together was safe and returned. She ran to their arms and they all stood embraced together. There were tears of joy and relief from them all. Julian was in the center of the embrace. He looked up as Mrs. Reed entered the room and stood in the doorway amazedly watching the reunion. He turned his eyes from her and looked out through the window to his beautiful, colorful, back garden. The dawn was just beginning to break. Nature was awakening. His world was safe and in Balance. He sensed the great Magic within him. It drew them all closer.

Then, looking deep into Darla's eyes he said:

"It is good to be with friends on such a sunrise."

She smiled lovingly,

"With friends."

She kissed him.

They were home.

About the Author

Terence Munsey lives in Richmond Hill, Ontario. He attended York University for undergraduate studies and then Stanford University for graduate studies, where he received an M.A. degree.

He has written five books in The Stoneman Series:

1. THE FLIGHT OF THE STONEMAN'S SON
2. THE KEEPER OF THREE
3. LABYRINTHS OF LIGHT
4. MARKS OF STONE
5. THEY OF OLD

He loves to hear from his readers. Send or fax him a letter.

E MAIL: terence_munsey@tvo.org,Internet

*Send $2.00 today and get your official 2&1/4in STONEMAN SERIES button.